Nicotine, Li...

Blasphemy

Richard Wall

Also by Richard Wall:

Fat Man Blues (Amazon, 2015)

Near Death (Burning Chair Publishing, 2020)

*"It's who I am
It's who I'll always be
Raised on Nicotine, Liquor,
and Blasphemy."*

From, 'Nicotine, Liquor, and Blasphemy'
Beelzebub Jones Ft. Half Deaf Clatch
© Speak Up Recordings 2018

v

Welcome to the inside of my head.

Foreword by Andrew McLatchie (aka Half Deaf Clatch)

I must admit I had reservations about writing this foreword, sometimes I have trouble getting my thoughts across, unless they're in the form of song lyrics. But I agreed, because Richard's writing deserves as much credit as humanly possible, and he promised he'd let me play his National Resonator guitar next time we meet. I'm honoured to be able to write a few words in praise of such a talented guy, and I'll do my best to get my thoughts across clearly, without resorting to rhyme.

The first time I came across Richard's writing was when he was promoting his first novel 'Fat Man Blues', a random twitter post caught my attention, I looked up the book, bought it – and loved it. And that was that, until Richard friend requested me on Facebook, we liked each other's posts (as is customary on social media), and it soon became apparent we had a very similar taste in music and humour.

Fast forward to 2018, and I randomly posted up a link to a new song I'd been working on in the style of a Spaghetti Western Soundtrack. Almost immediately Richard messaged me, saying he'd love to write a short story based on the ideas I'd laid down. The rest, as they say is history, we collaborated on three full albums over three years, Richard writing short stories for each one. You will find these dark western tales in the pages of this amazing compendium, along with other gems from the imagination of a truly great author.

During this very rewarding collaboration it became even more apparent that we shared the same dark sense of humour, and both loved a good play on words. It became a bit of a competition, to see who could come up with the best descriptive lines either as lyrics, or as part of the short story. The whole process of producing those albums was a lot more fun than anything should really be, and that was in no small part down to Richard's enthusiasm, commitment and ability as a wordsmith.

Pick any story or poem contained in these pages and his skill shines through, Richard has the rare gift of being able to paint a picture with only a few words, there is a skilful economy that lends itself effortlessly to his short stories and poems. The works in this book are an amazing example of Richard's creativity, imagination and humour. Sometimes thought provoking, always entertaining – this is a book that demands to be read and re-read.

Over the last few years, we've worked together on numerous projects, and helped each other out with different things, we've forged a lasting friendship built on creativity, humour and mutual respect. I look forward to whatever comes next, I know it'll be something special if Richard is involved.

Sharecropper

The idea for this has been bouncing around my head for a few years now. Thanks to Stu Cox for helping me keep it historically accurate, and Ran Walker for helping me to keep it real.
Don't try any of this at home.

Copiah County, Mississippi. 1943.

The mosquito whined past Chester Burnett's ear, settled on the back of his hand and then burst in an explosion of blood and insect matter.

Chester looked down, the scarlet mess on his calloused fingertips triggering memories of body parts scattered across a field in France.

Sweat, brought forth by the merciless heat of the afternoon sun, beaded like pearls against the ebony sheen of his forehead, swelled and then tracked slowly down his face.

Wiping his hands on the faded denim of his patched, frayed and dusty coveralls, images of 1918 faded as Chester lifted his eyes to stare at the

1

two white men sitting at a table just inside the doorway of a large wooden barn.

Behind them, dust motes hung in fingers of sunlight that poked through gaps in the roof to pick out various components of ancient farm machinery now reduced to junk.

A pitcher of lemonade pooled condensation onto the table as the white men made a big show of perusing the contents of a large, leather-bound ledger.

Ralph and Billy Dedman.

They held sway over the life of Chester and the other black sharecroppers on their land.

And they knew it.

Ralph, the elder brother, was thick set, stood about six-five and was the spit of his father, the recently deceased, "*Old Man*" Dedman.

Billy was a mean-spirited little runt. Nine inches shorter and fifty pounds lighter than Ralph, Billy made up for his physical inadequacies with a capacity for cruelty that was off the scale.

These two bastards would dictate how life would be for the next twelve months.

Chester watched as Ralph ostentatiously poured two glasses of lemonade, placing one next to Billy, who scribbled on a separate sheet of paper.

After a final check of the figures and a synchronised nod of agreement, Ralph snapped his fingers. "Step forward," he said.

"How's it going, Chester?" Billy's malicious smile spoke volumes about how it was about to go, but Chester kept his voice flat.

"Ain't too bad, Mistuh Dedman."

"Well," said Billy. "As you know, me and Ralph are running the place now."

Chester nodded. "I was sorry to hear about the passing of your father," he said.

"Oh, now you don't really mean that," said Billy. "I know for a fact that every negro for a hundred miles around talked about what a ornery sonofabitch he was."

"He still your father," said Chester. "Losing your Pa, it's like cutting a big hole in your heart. I remember when…"

Billy cut him off with a contemptuous wave. "I didn't ask you to make no goddam eulogy."

Chester stopped talking.

"Now," Billy said. "Because of the way things was left, there's gonna have to be a few changes to the way things are done aroun' here."

Here it comes.

"What kinda changes, suh?"

"Productivity, for one thing. There ain't no way to dress this up. You're just gonna have to pick more cotton next year."

"What's the other changes?" said Chester.

Billy's eyes danced with spiteful glee.

"We're going to have to look at how the income is shared out between us."

Chester kept his voice steady. "I'm already giving you two thirds of the cotton I pick, how much more you gonna take?"

Billy looked down at the figures and then back at Chester.

"Three quarters," he said. "And we gotta look at the rent on the land."

"Mister Dedman, suh. We struggling to get by as it is."

4

Billy shrugged. "That ain't our problem. The old man let things slide and now Ralph and me gotta pick up the pieces."

He paused.

"And we also gotta take a look at the new tools you're gonna need to buy."

"My tools is fine, ain't nothin' wrong with them."

"Your tools are old," said Billy. "Time you had some new ones. You're our tenant, it's only right that we make sure you got everything you need to pick more cotton."

Chester's heart hammered in his chest. "They my own tools, suh. I bought 'em myself when you was knee-high to a cricket."

"Sounds to me like you ready for a change, then," said Billy. "We got a good selection in our commissary and of course we'll give you the best discount we can."

Billy picked something from between his teeth, inspected it then wiped it down his shirt.

"Things gotta change, Chester," he said. "We need to get more machinery, so money's tight for all of us."

"I used to fix your pa's machinery," said Chester. "I could get it all working again so you don't have to spend no more. I…"

"This ain't a negotiation." The edge in Billy's voice was like a knife blade held to the throat.

Chester shook his head. Tried one more time.

"This ain't right, Mister Billy. We just cain't pick no more cotton. It's only me and my wife, and my daughters. When the cotton's high I gotta pay family or neighbours to come and help us as it is."

"We all gotta make sacrifices," said Billy. He paused as a feral expression crawled across his face.

"Speaking of your daughters, how old are they now?"

Chester paused, took a breath, tried to keep his voice flat. "Lucy, she ten; and Clara, she nearly fifteen."

"Young Clara, she sure growing up fast," said Billy. "She filling her clothes in all the right places."

His hands shaped an hour-glass in the air, and then he winked. "Maybe we can come to some kind of arrangement?"

Chester forced himself not to react. "What you mean?"

"Oh you know," winked Billy, his eyes glittering with malice. "If young Clara was nice to me now and then, maybe we could go a bit easier on your debts. Your little girl, she could be the answer to your problems."

A pause.

"She bleeding, yet?"

"Billy, for God's sake."

Billy looked at his brother in mock surprise. "What? I was only asking. These people talk like that all the time. It don't mean nothin'."

He turned to Chester. "Well? Is she?"

The tone of Billy's voice turned Chester cold inside.

He said nothing.

Billy stood up, stepped around the table, fronted up to Chester.

"I asked you a question, boy," he said. "Is she bleeding yet?"

Chester looked down at Billy, held his gaze. "You talkin' about my little girl, Mister Dedman. That ain't a nice thing to be saying."

For the first time in his life, Chester stared down a white man. The consequences filled him with dread, but at the same time a door opened inside him.

"Billy, stop being an asshole."

Ralph's voice broke the tension. Chester dropped his gaze and Billy stepped back.

"To get back to business," said Ralph. "We got a new agreement for you, for the terms we just spoke about. Valid for one year from today. Maybe next year we can look at making things easier for you. But that depends on you."

"Can I take it away and read it?"

"Of course you can," said Billy. "Right after you sign it."

Chester picked up the agreement, his heart dropping as he scanned the figures.

"Gimme the pen," he said.

*****

May Burnett handed her husband a bottle of Jax beer and sat next to him on the porch of their wooden shack.

"They got us bent over and they know it," Said Chester. "If I hadn't signed the agreement they'd a kicked us outta here befo' sundown."

"We can't work no harder," said May. "And we can't afford to give the Dedmans no more money."

"I told 'em that."

"So, what are we going to do?"

Chester took a sip of the beer. "Hell if I know," he said.

*****

The next afternoon, Chester was at the far edge of his plot, his eyes fixed on the hoe blade as it broke up the thin black soil, his mind trying to ward off dark memories.

He looked up at the sound of his name. Squinting against the low afternoon sun he made out a figure, a young man, hurrying in his direction, arms waving. As the young man drew closer Chester saw it was Buck Lawrence, eldest son of his neighbour.

Chester straightened, hands gripping the shaft of the hoe. "What's goin' on, Buck?"

Buck took a few seconds to catch his breath. "Misses Burnett sent me to gitchoo," he said. "Billy Dedman come around your place. You needs to..."

But Chester was gone, work boots kicking up dirt as he sprinted across the field. As he ran the rattle of machine-gun fire, the distant crump of artillery and the cries of the fallen played over and over in his head.

Minutes later he burst into the shack, chest heaving with exertion as he fought to make sense of the scene in front of him.

The room had been ransacked. The few possessions they had scattered across the floor, the table upended and chairs reduced to matchwood.

May, Lucy and Clara lay huddled together against the far wall. May looked up, her bruised face covered in congealed blood.

"What happened?" Chester said.

"Billy Dedman," May said, her voice flat. "Come round sayin' you was uppity and needed you some learnin'."

"What'd he do?"

"He grabbed a hold of Clara, tried to get his hand up her dress, I got in between 'em an' he hit me a couple times. He tried again with Clara so I jumped on him."

"Mama scratched his face," Lucy said. "So he called her a bitch. Said he's gonna burn us out." Lucy began to whimper, "I'm scared, Papa."

Chester knelt down next to her. "Ain't no need to be scared, baby girl. Ain't nobody gonna hurt us."

"We already been hurt."

Chester turned to look at Clara, for a moment fiercely proud of the defiance in her face. "Look what he done to Mama's face," she said. "He scared Lucy and tried to lay his hands on me."

"Don't argue with your father, Clara."

Clara flinched at her mother's scolding, but remained defiant. "I'm just telling Papa what's what."

"Best way we can deal with this is to be strong together," Chester said. "Now, you and your sister go draw some water, I'll get Mama back on her feet and we'll get her washed up."

Reluctantly, the two girls disentangled themselves, their faces sombre as Chester helped May stand up, and then guided her towards the small bedroom at the rear of the shack.

Sitting on the bed, May absent-mindedly stroked the iron framed footboard as she stared into the middle distance. A few moments later she turned to look at Chester, her face set in anger. "I wanted to kill the sonofabitch," she whispered. "When he grabbed a hold of Clara I tried to rip out his eyes." May lifted her right hand, showing Chester the blood congealing beneath her fingertips. "I raked his face," she said. "He go'n remember me ever'time he looks in the mirror."

Chester stroked her hair. "You paid a price though," he said. "An' Billy ain't gonna let that go."

"He left a message for you," said May. "He said if you let him be the first to take Clara, he'll rethink the terms of your contract."

Chester's fists bunched tight, cold rage coursing through his body. "If I *let* him…?"

"He wants you to go see him tomorrow," May said. "Wants you to look him in the eye and say it's OK for him to lay with your daughter." May paused. "That's what he told me to tell you. He said if he don't see you tomorrow morning at nine o'clock he gonna come here and make us watch as he takes Clara."

"The girls hear him say that?"

May nodded. "They was both holdin' on to me," she said.

They both looked up as Lucy walked in, followed by Clara carefully holding a large chipped-enamel bowl. "We got some hot water," Lucy said. "And a cloth to wash Mama's face."

Chester forced a smile. "You're good kids. Me and Mama, we glad to have you." He took the bowl from Clara, rested it on the bed then wrung a cloth in the water and began to wipe May's face.

When he'd finished, the water was stained red. "Take the bowl and go pour it outside," he said to Clara. "Take Lucy with you."

May turned to Chester. "What are we gonna do, honey?"

Chester sighed. "Guess I gotta go see Billy Dedman, see if we can get this sorted out."

*****

Next morning, at a quarter of nine, Chester drove his pickup into Dedman's yard and saw Ralph and Billy next to a barn, deep in conversation. He switched off the engine, took a deep breath then stepped out of the truck.

He wore a battered felt hat and as he walked towards the Dedman brothers he took it off and turned it nervously between both hands.

"Morning Chester," said Billy. His face twisted into a shit-eating grin. "You're early," he said.

14

"I like that in a man. Shows respect. Now, what've you got to say to me, boy?"

Chester kept his eyes on the ground, his hands trembling, his voice unsteady. "Mornin' Mister Dedman, suh," he said. "My wife told me what you said. I come to ask you to reconsider, suh," he said. "Clara, she my little girl and I don't wanna see her hurt."

"Maybe you should have thought of that before disrespecting me," said Billy. "You put yourself in this position. You ain't got nobody to blame 'cept yourself."

"I'm know that, suh," said Chester. "An I'm sorry, I truly am. I gets protective over my kids, was all. I didn't mean you no disrespect."

"Well," Billy said. "What's done's done. I'm giving you a way to make amend, you let me at your daughter and I'm prepared to let it go, and you can stick with last year's contract. I cain't say no fairer 'n that."

Chester dropped to his knees. "Please suh, she my little gal. Don't do this. I'll do anything. Please Mister Dedman, I'm begging you."

"Git up, now," said Billy. "You're making an exhibition of yourself. I told you what's gonna happen, and that's what's gonna happen." His smile grew wider. "But you gotta tell me it's OK."

"Billy," Ralph stepped forward. "Enough of this."

"Don't you question me," Billy snarled like a rabid dog, exuding a musk of barely-controlled violence. "These people need learnin'."

He turned back to Chester. "Get up off your knees and be a man. You know what I want you to say."

Chester stood. "Mister Dedman, please. Don't ask me to say that."

Billy stepped close enough for Chester to smell his rancid breath. "You're disrespecting me again. If you want you and your family to live beyond sundown, you'll damn well say it, boy."

Billy reached behind his back and then a Smith & Wesson .38 revolver was pressed hard against Chester's forehead.

"Say it, you sonofabitch."

Chester started shaking, his mind a confusion of terror and helpless rage. He took a breath, tried to disassociate himself.

"It's…" he began. Then dried up.

Billy's head tilted to one side. "Go on."

Chester tried again. "It's OK for you to come around."

The gun barrel pressed harder still.

"And?"

Chester's mind emptied in a finger-snap. Suddenly, everything was clear. He took another breath. "It's OK for you to come around and lay with my daughter."

Billy stepped back, lowered the .38 then slid it into the waistband of his pants. "There y'go," he said. "That wasn't so hard was it? I'll be around at sundown. Make sure she's ready."

Chester stared beyond Billy's head. Said nothing.

"You hear me, boy?"

Chester refocussed. "Yes suh, Mister Dedman."

Billy nodded. "That's more like it. Now git up and get along. I'm sure you got plenty of chores back home." He gave a dismissive wave then turned away.

When he'd gone, Chester turned to Ralph Dedman. "Please suh, cain't you do something? Talk to him maybe, tell him that this ain't right?"

"It's outta my hands," Ralph said. "You disrespected him. You can't expect him to let that go. You know what he can be like."

"But Mister Dedman, suh…"

"I said, NO." Ralph aimed his finger at Chester's face. "Actions breed consequences, you people would do well to learn that. What's gonna happen to your daughter was going to happen anyway at some point. May as well get it over with, and you never know, she might even enjoy it." Ralph paused. "Now, was there anything else?"

Defeated, Chester released a heavy sigh. "I got some things to take care of," he said. "I needs some tools and fixings. I got a list."

*****

That evening, Chester sat alone on the porch, a half-dozen empty Jax bottles scattered around his feet. Behind him stood a Victrola gramophone on which a record had just finished playing. Chester found comfort from the sound of the turntable mechanism gently winding down.

He cradled a fresh beer, deep in thought as he watched the sun paint the horizon in blood.

Slightly to his left a rooster tail of dust signified a vehicle approaching fast along the dirt road. A few moments later Billy Dedman's new Chevrolet pickup skidded to a halt in front of the porch.

Billy hopped out of the driver's door and skipped towards the porch steps. He stank of cheap cologne and Dapper Dan hair pomade. "What do you say, Chester?" He said. "Sure is a fine evenin' for it."

Chester nodded. "Evenin' Mister Dedman, suh," he said. then looked past Billy, watching as Ralph got out of the passenger door.

"Chester," said Ralph. "Me and Billy are going on into town afterwards, I'll just hang around here if that's OK?"

"Don't confront me none."

Billy rubbed his hands. "Well," he said. "Time's a wastin'. Where she at?"

Chester tipped his head. "She waiting for you in the back room."

"Guess I'll go right on in," Billy said. He jumped onto the porch, pulled the screen door open and went inside.

Ralph Dedman walked around to the front of the pickup, a Lucky Strike dangling from his lips as he searched for a book of matches.

The shotgun blast echoed from inside the shack, followed by the slump of a body and high-pitched shrieks of agony.

The Lucky Strike fell from Ralph's lips as he gaped first at the shack then at Chester.

"Get you a beer, Mister Dedman?" Chester lifted the bottle of Jax.

Ralph saw the flicker of sunset reflect from the fishing line tied around the neck of the

20

bottle, then two explosions from beneath the shack blasted lead shot into both his legs.

Ralph fell back on his ass, screaming in pain, his pants shredded from the knees down, blood and flesh from his ruined legs staining the dirt around him.

Inside the shack, Billy sobbed like a child, calling for Ralph to come help him.

Chester took a swig of beer, the smell of gunpowder, blood and raw meat reviving memories of 1918 as he watched Ralph somehow raise himself on hands and knees and begin to crawl towards the wooden steps, his legs dragging a bloody trail behind him.

"Come on up, Ralph," he said. "My house is your house, or is it the other way around?" Chester shook his head. "It don't matter, it ain't gonna be standing for much longer."

Whimpering in pain, Ralph Dedman reached the steps, began to drag himself upwards then paused, his chest on the porch, knees on the middle step. He looked like a shipwrecked sailor climbing onto a life raft. He turned to Chester,

"Please," he rasped. "Help me. I'll do whatever you want."

Chester winked then picked up an empty Jax bottle. Once again Ralph saw the fishing line then howled in agony as the gunshot, the sound muffled by his body, obliterated his groin and erupted a volcano of gore like a terminal fart from between the backs of his thighs.

Ralph slumped to the deck, chest heaving, each labored breath rattling in his throat as fresh blood poured down the steps.

"Now you know why I bought rat traps and fishing line this morning," said Chester. "Don't take much to make a homemade weapon. All you gotta do is auger a hole at the bait end of the trap, big enough to hold a 12-gauge shotgun shell; fix a firing pin to the hammer – I use gramophone needles from this ol' Victrola, they works a treat – and hey presto you got yo'self a booby trap."

Chester swigged a mouthful of beer. "I spent all day fixin' 'em around the place," he said. "Coverin' all eventualities, you might say."

He picked up another empty Jax bottle, saw Ralph flinch as the screen door exploded outwards inches above his head.

"I fixed one under the bedroom floor," Chester said. "Soon as Billy stepped into the room his dick was turned to Jell-O, just like yours. That's how come he howling so much."

Chester smiled, then lifted his head. "How you doing in there, Billy?" he called.

Billy moaned in reply. Chester nodded. "That's called reaping what you sow," he said. "Live by the sword you gonna die by the sword. Or in your case your pencil dick."

He turned back to Ralph. "You probably wondering what kinda sick mind would come up with the idea to make such a thing? Well, allow me to explain."

Chester tapped the side of his head. "I got demons inside of here," he said. "Had 'em since I come back from France. The ones I got from the war was bad enough, but I been getting more and more of them ever since, and they all belong to your old man. And now, cause of you and your brother, I

23

got a whole new set and I thought it's time you Dedmans had 'em all back."

He took another swig of beer, wiped his mouth on the back of his hand. "Believe me," he said. "But the monsters I got in my head right now, they ain't nothin'. See, when you a negro in Mississippi the biggest monster of them all is a white man. From the day I was born ever'thing in my life has been decided by a white man. I cain't see no further back than my grandparents cos they don't know nothin' beyond bein' slaves. I enlisted in the army to go fight the Germans. They sent me to France but Uncle Sam didn't want us fighting alongside white GIs."

Another swig of beer, followed by a soft belch. "So they had us doing jobs like Graves Registration. That's where you gotta walk around a battlefield, retrieving the bodies of dead GIs. Some of 'em been out there for days, weeks sometimes. Rotting and stinking. First one I seen was hanging off of barbed wire, his eyes pecked out by crows. Then I come across a poor sonofabitch in a bomb crater. I could see his head just sticking outta the water, guess his feet was stuck in the mud. I had to wade in and get him out. I grabbed a hold of his hand, gave a pull and fell backwards because his arm came right off at the shoulder. I had to stoop down, water up to my neck tryin' to get a hold of his body and drag him outta the crater. His papers said he was from South Carolina. I'd laid hands on a white boy like that back home, he'd a likely strung me up and set me on fire. Ain't that the dickens?"

Chester paused for a moment, stared up at the stars sprinkled like broken glass across the black asphalt of the night sky, then reached behind his chair and lifted a hurricane lamp and set it on the porch railing. Once lit, the kerosene hissed a yellow glow across the porch.

Chester set the lamp next to Ralph's head. Watched for a moment as flying insects began throwing themselves against the glass.

"After that I was sent to the 92nd Infantry Division. Buffalo Soldiers they called us, on account of the insignia we wore. We fought alongside the French on the Western Front at a battle called the Meuse–Argonne offensive. Treated us pretty good,

25

they did. And when we went into town on furlough the locals made us all feel welcome. Then we come home, some of us heroes and we had to go back to being treated like we just animals. We still can't go into a restaurant where white folks dine; still can't get a seat in a theatre where white people sit; or get a Pullman seat or a berth in a railroad car or even ride in a street car with white people. And we still getting lynched, just because we colored."

Chester shook his head. "Monsters is real, alright." He stood up, wound up the Victrola and gently positioned the needle over the record. There was a bump and the hiss of static and then the Mississippi night was filled with the descending guitar chords of *'Hellhound on My Trail'* by Robert Johnson.

Chester stepped over to Ralph's body, knelt down and slapped his cheek. "You still with us, Ralph?" he said.

Ralph looked up, his eyes pleading as he struggled to form words. "P'ease…" he whispered, blood dripping from his mouth. "P'ease have mercy."

"Soon enough," Chester said. He picked up the hurricane lamp, grabbed Ralph by the shirt collar and dragged him shrieking into the shack. Billy lay in the doorway to the bedroom. He was propped against the door frame, legs apart, sitting in a lake of blood. His groin turned to hamburger meat, his face disfigured beyond recognition.

"Worked better'n I thought it would," Chester said. "I knew he'd come struttin' in like a rooster so I rigged it that when Billy walked into the trip wire, it would fire upwards and the buckshot would hit him in the balls. Looks like some of it hit his face, too."

Chester positioned Ralph so that the brothers faced one another, then knelt between them. "I'm done playing Uncle Tom to the likes of white trash like you." he said. "Those words you made me say, did you think I was gonna let that go? Did you really think I was gonna let my little girl be polluted by your filth? Tonight my family's somewhere safe, and when I'm done with you sorry sonsabitches I'm gonna take your pickup, go and meet 'em up in Clarksdale and then we gonna take a

Greyhound to Chicago. By the time we get there this place gonna be a pile of ashes with what's left of you two motherfuckers lying right in the middle."

Chester stood, turned, walked into the kitchen then returned with a large gasoline can. Hefting the can into the crook of his arm, he unscrewed the cap then sloshed gasoline over the two bodies. Billy screamed as the fuel burned deep into raw flesh, blood rinsing from his face to reveal the extent of his disfigurement. Ralph leaned across, tried to grab Chester's ankle. "Please Chester," he croaked. "I'm begging you."

"You sayin' *Please* to me?" said Chester. His voice cold. "You *beggin'* me? How many times you ever say please to me in my life? How many times did I say please this morning when I knelt down and begged Billy not to rape my daughter?" He kicked Ralph in the face. "Please, my ass."

Chester poured more gasoline over the Dedman brothers, then used what was left to splash a trail out of the shack.

Out on the porch, as he listened to the Dedmans screaming for mercy, Chester rewound

The Victrola, dropped the needle, opened a book of matches and waited. When Robert Johnson began singing, Chester dropped a burning match into the trail of gasoline then stepped off of the porch.

The pickup had reversed a hundred feet when the shack erupted in a rolling fireball that sent flames leaping into the night sky.

The shack's aged, sunbaked timber burned with ferocious speed and intensity, but above the roar of the conflagration Chester could hear Robert Johnson singing about blues falling down like hail.

He took one last look at the burning shack, then put the Chevrolet truck into gear and headed to Clarksdale.

Evel Knievel and the Fat Elvis Diner

Back in the day I received an email on my non-smart phone. It took a long time to load, and for several minutes all I saw was a frustrating glimpse of half of a description in the Subject field. My imagination filled in the rest and hence this story was born.

The man stared through glass at the immense, dark thunderhead that filled the horizon.

Cumulonimbus.

Impressive.

Towering like a huge anvil in the vast Oklahoma sky. Even at this distance he could see the grey curtain of rain beneath it; threads of lightning poking at the earth like the antagonistic fingers of a spiteful child.

Cumulonimbus.

Majestic.

His phone beeped. He knew by the tone that he'd received an email, but he kept staring at the cloud.

Proper Okie storm on the way.

He looked down and touched the screen of the phone to open the mail inbox.

One new message.

He didn't recognise the sender and the subject line was empty, in the content pane were the words: *This guy w…*

The man frowned, peered closer.

This guy w…

He tapped the message, watched as it began to load then looked up.

He stared at the weather for a while then looked down again at the phone. The screen showed a rotating hour-glass.

This guy w…

Wasn't there a song called "This Guy"?

Who sang that? Was it Burt Bacharach?

No, don't think so. Sounds like something he might have written, though.

Who was it?

He snapped his fingers. Herb Alpert.

Good God.

Herb Alpert.

Flashback.

Nearly forty years.

Herb Alpert didn't sing very often but he got to Number One with this.

So dad said.

The man scowled.

Herb Alpert's singing now alright, an earworm cavorting round and round inside his head.

Fantastic.

It all came back, a slow, lazy trumpet riff.

Pah-Pah-Pa-Pahhhh, Pa-PAH-Pah-Pa-Pa-Pahhh.

Music you'd hear in a lift, or a shopping centre, or an old folk's home.

What the hell are those dad?

Leave it, son. Please.

Music you'd hear when a call centre puts you on hold.

Pa-PAH-Pah-Pa-Pa-Pahhh.

For God's sake.

The man rubbed his eyes, tried to get the song out of his head. He looked down at the phone.

Rotating hour-glass.

Probably a bunch of photos, or a movie.

This guy w…

Tijuana Brass.

Yellow album cover. Dog-eared cardboard. Pictures of trumpets.

England, 1970's.

Childhood.

Dad's record collection: Herb Alpert and the Tijuana Brass, George Formby, Glenn Miller, Jim Reeves, Ray Conniff.

Dear God.

Ray Conniff.

The man shook his head. How many times did we have to listen to Ray flaming Conniff and his singers blasting through the house?

Each to their own, of course, but for a small boy it was easy-listening hell.

God save the Sex Pistols.

1970's.

K-Tel Records.

K-Tel adverts on the black and white tv.

What was that thing? Oh yeah, the Buttoneer. Fixed buttons just like magic. Imagine that on Dragon's Den; I'll tell you where I am, I'm out.

The Buttoneer.

Was that K-Tel, or was it Ronco?

Why do I care?

Pa-PAH-Pah-Pa-Pa-Pahhh.

AHHHHHH.

Screaming helped a little. But not much.

The man sighed and looked at his watch. Another hour yet.

Tijuana Brass.

Childhood.

What's Tijuana, Dad?

Somewhere ruddy foreign.

Ruddy. Dad's favourite word.

Any place further than twenty miles away was "*ruddy foreign.*"

Thanks, Dad.

So, he'd looked it up for himself. Went to the library, found a Readers Digest World Atlas and discovered that Tijuana is a town in Mexico, on the Pacific coast just over the border from San Diego, California. To a small-town kid on a council estate in the sticks, these places sounded exotic.

The man grunted.

Exotic.

He went to San Diego with the navy. Took the tram to San Ysidro and walked across the bridge into Tijuana to see for himself. Ended up in the Zona Norte, the North Zone, where the only thing remotely exotic was the medical condition that he contracted from the Mexican hooker he picked up in a shabby, down at heel bar. After drinking his body weight in tequila, he waved her over and they went upstairs, while a mariachi band played in the street. Got into trouble for that alright. Self-inflicted injury, the navy called it.

Seemed like a good idea at the time.

When in Rome and all that.

Mind, she was fit.

Exotic.

He looked down at the phone.

This guy w…

Rotating hour-glass.

Loading content.

This is taking a while, must be the weather. Better be good, whatever it is.

He reached for the packet of Lucky Strikes, took

one out, lit it, took a long drag then blew bored smoke rings.

Staring through glass. Thinking.

Growing up in the 1970's.

Morecambe and Wise Christmas Special. Patch Pockets. Champion the Wonder Horse. The Sweeney. The hot summer of '76. The Austin Allegro. Clackers. Action Man.

You ain't havin' an Action Man.

Please, dad.

Not a chance.

Corgi Toys.

Receiving, as a birthday gift, a die-cast model of a 1970 Dodge Challenger, the one from the movie 'Vanishing Point'.

Capturing his imagination like nothing else. A glimpse into another world that ignited a life-long obsession.

For a small boy, the closest thing to falling in love. American muscle cars.

Proof that God exists, engines have souls and heaven is in Motor City.

Dodge Challenger.

Standing still it looked like it was doing a hundred miles an hour.

Then one day, reading the Daily Mirror and seeing that 'Vanishing Point' was being shown on TV.

Begging his dad to let him stay up and watch it.

Drinking in every second of the movie. Entranced at the sight of the beautiful car bellowing across the American landscape to the soundtrack of Delanie and Bonnie and Friends.

Typical Yanks. Ruddy far-fetched.

Yeah, but look at the car, dad. That's a Dodge Challenger.

Ruddy Yank tank. I'd rather have the Jag.

Didn't even own a car, back then.

Why can't we have a car, dad?

There ain't no point. If I bought one I'd only have to ruddy drive it.

Can't argue with that logic.

Had to make do with a Raleigh Chopper.

Every penny from the paper round went to paying for that. A pound a week to the neighbour who ran a Kay's catalogue. Probably dead now. What was her name?

Hilda something.

The man smiled, then laughed out loud.

Pretending to be Evel Knievel. Imagination transformed the Raleigh Chopper into the Skycycle X-2, chalk lines on the road marked the Snake River Canyon and two breeze blocks and a plank made the launch ramp.

"Whilst undoubtedly a creative and imaginative student, he fails to apply these qualities to his schoolwork and this is reflected in his poor academic results. He has trouble concentrating and is easily distracted…"

Riding the Chopper 100 yards down the road, locking the back wheel to skid round in a perfect one-eighty, like Steve McQueen in The Great Escape, and then taking a second to savour the atmosphere. The council estate became southern Idaho, kids from the estate became fans, imaginary cheers filling the air whilst overhead a lone eagle calls a lonesome *Screeee* as it circles lazily on thermals above the canyon. A deep breath and a brief nod to the crowd then setting off and pedalling fast, notching the T-shaped lever from first to second and then up to third gear, kids becoming a blur but seeing dad in the front garden, the Chopper hitting

39

the ramp, flying through the air, bouncing hard on the huge back tyre, losing control and demolishing Hilda-something's wooden fence.

Thought dad was going to have a stroke, he laughed so hard.

That hurt, dad.

That'll learn ya.

The man smiled again. Every accident, mishap or minor injury was met with the same response.

Watcha cryin' for now?

Fell out of a tree, dad.

That'll learn ya'.

Pa-PAH-Pah-Pa-Pa-Pahhhh.

The ear worm was still alive.

Give me strength.

The 1970's.

The music.

Melody Maker. New Musical Express. Record Mirror.

September 1976.

Skiving off school and catching the train to London with a mate whose uncle worked at the 100 Club.

What the ruddy hell were you thinking of? Your mum was

ruddy demented.

International Punk Festival.

Subway Sect. Whatever happened to them? Siouxsie and The Banshees, The Clash.

The Sex Pistols.

Ever get the feeling you've been had?

Other concerts. Mohicans, spitting, safety-pins, pogo dancing, stage-diving. A fat kid, airborne; captured by the strobe lights and held in the air for a split second, the crowd parting like the Red Sea, the expression on his face.

The cheer when he hit the floor.

'White Riot' at maximum volume, dad storming into the bedroom.

Why do you have to play it so ruddy loud?

It's The Clash, dad.

Ruddy noise if you ask me, ruddy turn it down will ya'?

Other bands, other gigs. The Buzzcocks, The Stranglers, The Clash again, still got the ticket from that one. What a night.

It's up to you not to heed the call-up.

Good times.

The storm cloud was moving closer. Lightning

flashes becoming more dramatic. Curtain of rain almost filling the sky.

Proper Okie storm.

Oklahoma.

Dad's reaction.

What the ruddy hell do you want to go there for? Full of ruddy Yanks.

Thanks, dad.

No inclination to travel. Not interested in foreign food.

Want some curry, dad?

Wouldn't give ya' a thank ya for it. Ruddy mixed-up tack.

Got his news from the Daily Mirror and his social life playing crib at the local on a Wednesday night.

Same routine.

Week after week after week.

As a kid, it was a mystery. There were places called Denver, San Diego, Tijuana and Detroit - where they built muscle cars. A whole world of exotic places. Why would anyone want to stay in such a miserable, grey, insular, rural existence in the back end of nowhere?

He'd never understood.

Until he'd left home and been through a war of his own. Seen at first hand the things that humans could do to each other.

Two bombs dropped on a ship in the South Atlantic.

Watching helplessly as your best mate burned to death in front of you.

His screams in your nightmares.

Your screams when you wake.

Detachments to Bosnia, Iraq, Afghanistan.

After that he understood.

Understood that if you're a twenty year old kid and you get your call-up papers and for the first time in your life you've got to leave the small country town where you were born and raised, put on a uniform and then spend the next five years fighting halfway across the planet before they'll let you go back home – in one piece if you were lucky – and during those five years all you saw was suffering, death, bloodshed and destruction, if you made it home, why would you ever leave again?

Who could blame you for staying put?

Proper infantry fighting, too. Back then.

Like it is now.

Never mind your, over-the-horizon, fire-and-forget technology.

Never mind your precision air-strikes.

None of that for the blokes on the ground.

No siree, Bob.

What did dad used to say?

Poor ruddy infantry.

Just you, a Lee Enfield .303, a bayonet and your pals behind you.

House to house. Hand to hand. Look the other bloke in the eye and hope you can kill him before he kills you. Day after day after day.

Twenty years old.

Kill him before he kills you.

Like it is now.

Poor ruddy infantry.

Never understood.

Until that day in the old folks home.

Never seen dad undressed. Never even saw him without a shirt.

Until that day.

The day he'd walked in while the care assistant was giving his dad a wash. Eastern European, she was, smiling and stroking his head. Making time for him. Compassion on a weekly wage that no British person would get out of bed for.

The day he'd walked in and saw the scars for the first time, the puckered circle just below his left shoulder, two more on his back, the slice marks across the stomach.

His dad crossing his thin, bony arms, trying to cover his wasted body like a bashful virgin. Ashamed.

Jesus Christ! What the hell are those dad?

Nothin'.

Dad?

I don't want to talk about it.

But dad?

Leave it, son. Please.

Dad getting agitated.

The care assistant putting her arms around him. Genuine affection in her eyes as she whispered soothing words in her native language, calming him down.

I never hugged him.

And then, clearing the house after dad died. Finding the medal and the letter from the King. The conversation with his uncle at the funeral, the story no one else knew.

Poor ruddy infantry.

My dad, the hero. And he never said a word.

I never hugged him.

Cried his eyes out the day I joined the navy.

So mum said.

You ain't getting an Action Man.

The storm cloud grew closer.

A single, fat raindrop hit the glass. Then another.

Oklahoma storm.

Oklahoma City? What the ruddy hell do you want to go there for?

Cos Chuck Berry says it's pretty.

Do what?

Chuck Berry, dad. Sang a song about Route 66.

Ruddy noise if you ask me.

Not like Ray Conniff, eh dad?

Oklahoma.

Had enough with the navy.

Fancied something different.

Came to America, no plans.

Bought a muscle car, a white 1970 Dodge Challenger

R/T. 440 cubic inches, just like in the movie.

The real deal. It'll pass anything except a gas station.

What else? If you're gonna be a bear, be a grizzly.

Stamp on the loud pedal and it howls like a banshee and leaps forward like an attack-dog. Awesome in a straight line. On a corner, forget it.

A barely-tamed monster of a car.

Caned it across America, just like Kowalski in Vanishing Point. Arrived in Yukon, Oklahoma and met a waitress in The Fat Elvis diner.

Beautiful smile.

Beautiful lady.

Apple pie and cream.

Ah love yo' accent, honey.

And I love yours.

Aw hell, I don't have no acc-ey-ent.

What time do you get off, beautiful lady?

The nightmares stopped that night.

Married a week later, imagine that?

Three years and two kids ago and still together. Still got the car, too.

Thinking about her made him smile.

He looked down at the phone.

Photographs began appearing.

About time.

He reached across to the ashtray, stubbed out the cigarette and looked closely at the screen.

A bunch of people standing at the side of a road.

A cop standing next to his patrol-car.

To Protect and Serve.

He scrolled down to the next photo.

Grim-faced emergency workers looking down at something out of camera view.

Next photo.

Like a still from a Tarantino movie.

A blood-soaked corpse lying on a plastic sheet next to a pile of twisted metal.

The man looked closer.

Correction, half a blood-soaked corpse. The victim, a young man, had been torn in half at the waist, ripped flesh and entrails fanning out from his stomach cavity. Shocked expression on his face.

Not surprised.

Next photo.

Emergency workers wearing blood-stained vinyl gloves, gripping the victim's ankles as they dragged the lower half of his body from the wreckage. Gore trailing from the waist.

Next photo.

Both halves of the victim dumped on the plastic sheet, like a broken, shop-window mannequin.

Like a broken Action Man.

Next photo.

Two vehicles. Head-on collision.

The back end of an SUV sticking out from the radiator grill of a huge Kenworth truck.

Blimey, must have been going some.

Looked like the truck was eating the car.

The Fat Elvis Diner.

Apple pie and cream.

I don't have no acc-ey-ent.

Beautiful smile.

Beautiful lady.

"This guy's in love with you."

The man scrolled back to the previous photos.

Looked in fascination at the carnage laid out on black plastic.

That'll learn ya.

Scrolled to the top of the message.

Read the first line.

"This guy was reading an email whilst driving."

The man heard the blast of the horn.

Looked up through the rain-covered windshield of the 1970 Dodge Challenger.

Saw the radiator grill of the huge Kenworth truck.

Drivin' with Mr. D

This is a short tale about the bloke who drives the Grim Reaper around. Michael Clark, a supremely talented writer from the USA, agreed to film himself narrating it. The video is available on my YouTube channel.

Mr. D, he tells me where we gotta go.

Most folks get it. They kinda nod and get in without any fuss.

Those who don't, they try to argue.

Or beg.

But it don't make no difference.

The end is always the same.

Sitting next to Mr. D, in the back seat of a 1954 Pontiac Star Chief.

It ain't a long journey. Just a coupla blocks.

Matter of fact, it don't matter where you are in the world, it's always just a coupla blocks, and the same destination: a multi-storey parking garage in the French Quarter in New Orleans.

Now, I growed up in New Orleans and I told Mr. D I ain't never seen no garage in the French Quarter.

Mr. D, he just smiled and told me I ain't been looking in the right place.

Anyhow.

What happens is, I pull into the entrance. In front of me there's two barriers.

I flash my headlights and one of the barriers will lift. If it's the one on the right then that means the up-ramp, a concrete spiral that leads on up to the roof. It's kinda hard to explain what it's like up there. You come off the ramp and out into a bright, white mist. Like the fog comin' off of the Mississippi river, but it ain't cold and it ain't wet.

I stop the car and I get out and open the door. The white mist gets kinda thinner and shapes begin to emerge, figures that walk a few steps, raise their arms in welcome and then gather around the passenger and walk 'em back into the mist.

It's kinda peaceful.

When we got children in the car they always goes up to the roof.

It ain't heaven. That's a notion invented by man. Mr. D told me that.

He said earth-bound religion is what keeps me and him so busy.

Where was I?

Oh yeah.

If it's the barrier on the left that raises, well, you can guess where that leads to.

Down to level nine. A place so dark it smothers my headlights.

It's an evil kind of dark. The kind that would cut your throat just to watch you bleed.

First time I drove down there I nearabout messed my pants. Couldn't see a damn thing.

Mr. D told me where to stop. Told me to stay in the car.

The client was a preacher. Started to moaning and crying and repenting and such.

Mr. D told him to get outta the damn car.

The preacher got his ass out.

Shapes appeared. Shapes so black they stood out in the absolute darkness. I heard a scream and then the preacher was gone.

I done some bad things in my time. Some very bad things. But after that first time down on level nine I told Mr. D that I was sorry for every damn one of 'em. Said I was sorry for all the people I hurt. Said I didn't want to end up like the preacher.

Mr. D said, "That's OK, son. You jus' keep drivin' this big ol' Pontiac."

Blue-eyed American Jesus

I love America. Always have done. But, like every nation, it has its issues. This was inspired by (yet another) mass shooting.

I got a blue eyed, American Jesus,
In a picture on my trailer wall,
He's been talking to me while I'm sleepin',
Since I's baptised in the river, y'all.

I don't believe in no evolution,
It was God who created this land,
I got schooling from my momma's bible,
And the belt in my daddy's right hand.

My momma gives dollars for Jesus,
To a preacher she seen on TV,
I seen him get into a black limousine,
Windows dark so he couldn't see me.

My ten-year-old sister she's pregnant,
Daddy said, 'Well, it must be God's will,'
My sister told me that she doesn't want it,
But the bible says, *'thou shall not kill'*.

Preacher says it's an a-bom-in-ation,
For a man to lie down with a man,
Jesus told me to do something about it,
While I's sleeping he told me his plan.

55

He said, "Hell, boy, those queers need a lesson,
I know where they meet up, and so,
Get your AR-15 fully loaded,
With spare magazines, ready to go."

"Fire up that old Chevrolet pickup,
And drive it on down to the mall,
And think of blue-eyed American Jesus,
As you watch all those deviants fall."

"And you see that young, brown middle-eastern?,
He looks like a terrorist for sure,
Shoot him six times with your rifle, son,
Then six more as he bleeds on the floor."

Jesus told me that I'm patriotic,
Told me what I was doing was right
He said, "We need Christian soldiers like you,
To git out there and fight the good fight."

Now the blue eyed, American Jesus,
Is up on my prison cell wall,
Tomorrow I talk to the preacher man,
Then I'll finally meet Jesus, y'all…

The Red Button

This story is about a woman and a red button.

She looked at the red button and then at her watch.

Fifteen minutes to go.

Funny how the mind works. Up until this morning her head was filled with a maelstrom of conflicting thoughts, 'what-ifs?', hopes, prayers and regrets.

But now the storm had passed, her mind had emptied and her world had distilled to contemplation of a small, innocuous push-button.

Events of the past few weeks had moved rapidly out of her control, to the point that she had realised that the simple act of pressing the button might well be the last decision she would ever make for herself. A simple, physical act that would initiate a chain of events that would change things forever.

Fourteen minutes to go.

She stared at her wristwatch. The smooth motion of the second-hand reminded her of the sweep of a radar screen in a war movie; tension building with each revolution.

No contacts.

Recently her mind had taken her to some very dark places. A recurring theme had been, "What will the final moments be like? When will people begin to forget what I look like, struggle to remember my name and finally forget that I ever existed?"

After watching three minutes disappear from her life she looked up at the red button and took comfort from its bland, inert simplicity.

"*I'm here*," it seemed to say. "*Ready to change your life whenever you are.*"

She cursed inwardly at the absurdity of it all. It's just a button, that's all.

Nevertheless, her pulse-rate increased at the prospect of what was about to happen. A band of anxiety tightened across her chest and for a brief moment she allowed herself a pang of loneliness at having to face this on her own.

She cursed again. Far too late for self-pity, regret or self-recrimination.

We are where we are.

Ten minutes to go.

She stared at the button.

The button stared back.

Difficult not to be angry, though. Anger at herself and the realisation that spending so long with her head in the sand had achieved nothing, helped no one.

Ain't that the truth?

She inhaled and let out a deep, cleansing sigh. No point dwelling on it. Just have to face up to the fact that what's done is done and growing smaller in the rear-view mirror. Have to look ahead, one step at a time; all those good clichés that get trotted out.

Her watch informed her gleefully that time was running out and that she had eight minutes to go. The red button waited patiently, as if quietly self-assured of the significance of the part it would play in the next act of her life drama.

Her pulse thumped faster as she felt the stirrings of another mind-storm. Closing her eyes she inhaled and exhaled slowly, breathing from the stomach in an attempt at a calming technique she had learned from a yoga website.

Desperate times call for desperate measures. Gradually, her heartbeat slowed and she began to relax.

Opening her eyes, she squinted and moved her head to inspect the button from different perspectives. She wondered where it was made. Was there a factory somewhere that made red buttons? Who made this one and what was he or she doing right now? Probably making more red buttons whilst surreptitiously keeping one eye on the clock, counting the minutes until they could go home to their family.

One eye on the clock.

Five minutes to go.

She wondered how many red buttons that person made each day and what he or she would say if they could see the emotions this one was stirring up.

Pointless questions, but calming nonetheless, a helpful distraction that almost helped her forget.

Almost.

Three minutes to go.

She shivered as a blast of irrational fury swept through her, causing her to shake with bitter resentment towards the person who made this red button. Joe or Josephine Average leading a normal, everyday existence, free from life-or-death decisions.

How dare they?

As quickly as it arose, her rage abated, a momentary squall just passing through.

Nothing to see.

Soon be over, one way or another.

Two minutes to go.

She closed her eyes again, breathed deeply as she tried once more to calm herself.

In a single, unconscious movement, she placed her right hand beneath her left breast, her fingers going straight to the hard, round lump, as they had every day since she found it twelve months ago. In that instant she relived the year of fear and sleepless nights as it continued to grow and the

61

overriding emotion of self-denial; ignoring it stubbornly until last month when she began to feel ill and an internet search of her symptoms gave her the courage to visit her doctor.

She remembered also the look on his face as he examined her, his expression betraying the casual way in which he made the emergency appointment, his polite but urgent insistence that she was to be seen straightaway and then the hollow feeling inside when the oncologist gave her the results of the scan.

He was cagey when she asked what her chances were, but deep down she knew.

They wouldn't know the full picture until they opened her up, he said. But there was no time to lose.

Time.

Her eyes blinked open. She looked around, took a final glance at her watch and then focused on the button.

It was time.

Taking a deep breath, she lifted her hand and noted the slight tremor as she extended her finger.

The red metal button felt cold to the touch and resisted only slightly before succumbing to her insistent pressure.

She felt the contact but still jumped when the bell rang out loud and clear.

It was over.

And here she was.

She looked at the red button then stood up as the bus slowed to a halt outside the entrance to the hospital.

The Kidney Punch

Based on a true story, this tale is set in 1983 onboard the
nuclear submarine HMS Colossus, somewhere beneath the
North Atlantic.

"Stand-by to surface!"

Cocooned in the warmth of his sleeping bag,
Able Seaman Dave "Dinger" Bell opened his eyes
and blearily checked his watch.

22:30, two more hours to go. Happy days.

A submarine crew is split into two watches,
known as First Watch and Second Watch. First
Watch work 7 o'clock to 1 o'clock, Second Watch 1
to 7.
Six hours on, six hours off the whole time at sea,
sometimes for months on end. This meant that sleep
time was precious and Dave lay awake just long
enough to feel the boat begin to roll and then smell
the foul odour of fresh air before falling back to
sleep to the muffled sound of a helicopter.

He woke again to someone shaking his leg, then a voice hissed, "Dinger." Then more insistent shaking followed by a louder hiss, "DINGER!"

Dave rolled over, opened his eyes and was temporarily blinded by a flashlight at full beam, held by a grown man giggling like a child.

"Bastard!"

"Time to get up, mate."

Dave clambered out of his bunk, staggered to the bathrooms, freshened up and then joined the queue for the galley and some home-made soup.

"What's in the soup, chef?"

"Fucked if I know."

"Happy with that."

Sitting in the mess with a mug of indeterminate contents and a thick hunk of bread, Dave looked around at a dozen sailors avidly watching a porn video featuring multiple participants writhing, gasping, moaning and screaming to a 1970's, *boom-chicka-wah-wah* soundtrack.

Dave grinned, "What's the movie about?"

No response.

"Is there a car chase?"

"Fuck off, Dinger."

Dave laughed, finished his soup, rinsed his mug and made his way along the semi-dark passageway, climbed a ladder and turned to his left.

The Control Room was lit in an eerie red glow, referred to imaginatively as 'red-lighting', as it was every night at sea. Before raising the periscope at night, all lights would be switched-off resulting in pitch-darkness known equally imaginatively as 'black-lighting'. The transition from red to black-lighting helped the captain maintain his night-vision when using the periscope and was also the source of endless amusement for a bored crew by providing the perfect cover for a sick mind to deliver an anonymous, random kidney-punch.

Able Seaman "Knocker" White was the unofficial 2nd Watch kidney-punch champion and arch nemesis of Dave. Standing a full five-feet-six inches in his smelly socks and proud owner of a 'fuller-figure' maintained religiously by a diet of beer and kebabs, Knocker had brought Dave to his knees more times than he could remember by a sudden blow to his lower back that brought tears to his eyes and emptied his lungs of air.

Tonight, Knocker was at his usual position standing in front of a display and Dave eyed him warily as he threaded his way through the dimly-lit control room and walked into the Sonar Room.

"What's happening?" he said.

The Sonar Petty Officer turned to Dave. "We're coming up to PD in a few minutes to mix it up with a few skimmers."

In English this meant that the submarine was going rise to periscope-depth and carry out a series of simulated attacks on some Royal Navy warships. There was no love lost between submariners and skimmers.

Dave put on headphones and settled down at his sonar set.

The captain's voice barked over the tannoy, "Black lighting in the control room, stand by to return to periscope depth."

The submarine responded with a slight bow-up angle and the next couple of hours passed in a blur of activity as the captain maneuvered the submarine to engage multiple targets in a game of cat and mouse. This kept the operations team busy as they had to listen out for the constant changes in depth, course and speed and adjust their sensor equipment accordingly.

After two and a half hours, the Petty Officer tapped Dave on the shoulder. "Looks like things are gonna be quiet for a while, Dinger. Go and get yourself a cuppa and be back here in fifteen minutes."

Dave nodded and walked out of the Sonar Room. Standing for a second to allow his eyes to adjust to the almost pitch darkness of the control room, Dave noticed a familiar portly shape hunched over a faintly glowing screen and allowed himself a terrible grin.

Knocker White was still there. Payback time.

With the stealth of a panther, Dave crept over to stand behind the diminutive, rotund shape presently engrossed in the goings-on of the electronic display.

Thank you, God.

Adjusting his stance and taking a deep breath, Dave flexed his shoulders, curled his right hand into a tight fist with the middle knuckle protruding, swung his arm back into the middle of last week and let go.

It was the punch of a heavyweight champion, the strike of an assassin. With the speed of an arrow leaving a bow, Dave's fist shot forward with unerring accuracy, burying itself knuckle-deep in soft doughy flesh just below the rear of the victim's rib cage.

The response was immediate. Dave winced at the sound of the head hitting the display screen, but grinned triumphantly as the figure sank to his knees moaning in pain.

Biting his fist to quell hysterical laughter, Dave made good his escape, moving as a shadow through the darkened control room with the swiftness of a ninja. He was elated. Best kidney-punch, ever.

Exiting the control room, Dave descended the ladder and made his way to the mess. He was still laughing maniacally as he walked into the mess.

There, nursing a cup of tea, sat Knocker White.

Dave did a classic Hollywood double-take. "What the fuck are you doing here?"

"Havin' a cup of tea," said Knocker.

"Who's on your display, then?"

"Rear Admiral Harrison," said Knocker. "Little fat fucker, just like me. He came onboard when we surfaced last night, said he joined the navy as a boy seaman and wanted to have a go at being an operator again."

Knocker paused. "Why do you ask?"

Just then the loudspeaker clicked.

"Able Seaman Bell, report to the control room...NOW!"

Finding Pops McCoy

*In the 1950s and 1960s white blues enthusiasts went door to
door in Black neighbourhoods in Mississippi, buying up
78rpm blues recordings for a few cents each.
Those records are now worth tens of thousands of dollars.*

It was three in the afternoon when Charlie
called. I was sitting on a stool made from an old
tractor seat, at the bar of the "Wormy Dog" Saloon
in Oklahoma City, and getting outside of my fourth
Budweiser.

"I found him," said Charlie.

"Found who?" I said.

"Pops McCoy."

I was skeptical.

Let me explain.

Henry 'Pops' McCoy was an old delta
bluesman. Born in 1920 in a shotgun shack just
outside Clarksdale, Mississippi, he was a left-handed
albino, blind in one eye, who played a mean guitar
and made money wandering around playing the
blues at fish-fries and juke joints across Mississippi.

Story goes he cut ten recordings in the 1930s and then disappeared.

Only one photograph of him exists and only one of his records was ever found, supposedly kept in the vault of an anonymous collector and last valued at ten big ones.

Yep, you heard me right, ten thousand dollars.

For over four decades, blues historians who discovered Son House, Skip James, Bukka White and Furry Lewis, have searched for Pops McCoy with no success and now my college drop-out buddy and fellow blues freak tells me he's found the Holy Grail.

"Where's he buried?" I said, taking a sip of beer.

"He ain't dead."

Budweiser sprayed across the bar.

"Get the fuck outta here."

Charlie was beside himself. "It's true man. Get this, he's livin' in Okarche, Oklahoma."

"That's on the way to Kingfisher, right?"

"Yeah, imagine that, a blues legend livin' an hour away."

"He must be like, 98," I said. "How the hell did you find him?"

"My sister told me."

Charlie had my undivided attention.

"Run that by me again?" I said.

"OK, it's like this," said Charlie. "My sister Babs, she moved out to Okarche a coupla years back. Well, she just got herself a volunteer job helping out senior citizens, you know, delivering food, cleanin' up around the house, shit like that."

"OK."

"So, anyway, she tells me she's met this ancient dude, well into his nineties, calls himself 'Pops' an' keeps goin' on about when he played the blues; talks about seein' Charley Patton and Robert Johnson play when he was a kid. Babs thinks he ain't all there but she says he's got a beat up ol' gittar he picks on now and then."

"So he calls himself Pops an' plays the gittar," I said. "Don' mean it's Pops McCoy."

"That's true," said Charlie. "McCoy ain't his given name, it's Smith or some bland shit like that, but I asked her what the dude looked like."

"And?"

"And she said he's an albino an' he's got a milky eye an' he plays the gittar left-handed." Charlie laughed. "Best of all, she sent me a picture of him playin' the gittar. It's him, man. I know it's him."

"What do you wanna' do?" I said.

"I'm comin' round to pick you up, we're goin' up there tonight. You better be sober, dude."

That night we stopped at Babs' house in Okarche. She said she thought Pops' mind was pretty much shot to shit and all he talked about was the old days in Mississippi. She also said that she saw a box containing five 78rpm records, each with a Paramount Records label.

I looked at Charlie.

Back in the sixties when the blues became popular, collectors would walk the black neighborhoods of Mississippi, knocking on doors and buying up old records. By the seventies, pretty much every decent record had been found and that's when the prices started going up.

Original Paramounts were rare. Very rare indeed.

Between us we reckoned we could raise about eight-thousand bucks. Charlie said we should offer five and see where things went.

Next day, the three of us arrived at a tiny wooden house on the outskirts of town. Babs knocked on the door. After a few minutes, a frail old man appeared, stooped over a walking frame, and dressed in grey jogging pants and a plaid bathrobe. "Hey Pops," said Babs. "How're you doing? I've brought my brother and his friend to see you." Pops smiled in vague recognition. "Well come on in," he said.

"You folks go on and sit down," said Babs. "I'll go into the kitchen and get us something to drink." We followed Pops into a room that smelled of old age. He waved us to a threadbare sofa, and then lowered himself into a battered armchair.

Once settled, a cloud of confusion passed over his face. "Who you folks again?"

"Fans of yours, sir," said Charlie. "Babs is my sister."

We talked about the blues for a while, his face became alive as he spoke of the old days, but then his voice tailed off, his good eye staring into the distance as his mind closed down.

Then he came back.

"Who you folks say you were?"

When we told him again, he said, "Oh yeah, tha's right, y'all come t'look at my recuds."

Pops waved to a cardboard box in the corner of the room. "Drag tha'n over, son."

I picked up the box and carried it back to the sofa, my hands trembling as I pulled out and examined each record.

They looked the real deal. Five 78 discs in almost pristine condition.

"Recorded them in Grafton, Wisconsin in nineteen an' thirty-seven." Said Pops.

"Well sir," said Charlie. "We was wonderin' if you'd be thinkin' of sellin' them?"

Pops frowned. "Y'all wanna buy them scratchy ol' things?"

"Yes sir," said Charlie. "An' we'd pay you a lot of money."

"S'at right?" said Pops. "An' how much is a lot of money?"

"Well," Charlie said. "We got five thousand dollars in cash."

Pops whistled. "Five thousand dollars?"

He fell silent, staring into the middle distance for a long time.

Charlie blinked first. "Of course, we might be able to move it up a notch."

Pops came back. "Yo'd pay more than five thousand?"

"Yes sir," said Charlie. "How much was you thinking of?"

The old man sighed, and then scratched his chin.

"Well," he said. "I was thinkin' of fifty-thousand dollars."

On Days Like These

This is inspired by the opening scene to one of my all-time favourite films, 'The Italian Job'. It's a work of fiction, Simon Faith did not appear in the film.

Aosta, The Italian Alps. 1969

What happened?

Simon Faith sat at the edge of the mountain road, staring down the ravine at the twisted remains of the 1968 Lamborghini Muira burning fiercely on a rocky outcrop fifty feet below.

The last thing he remembered was entering the tunnel, windows open to get the full effect of the glorious sound of the V12 engine. Then the smell of petrol, the whoomph as it ignited, smoke filling the cabin; then the impact and the sensation of the car spinning out of control.

Simon turned, saw the strips of rubber on the asphalt, interspersed with metallic scrapes and flakes of orange paint showing where the Muira had spun, rolled and then left the road. He looked back down into the ravine.

I must have been thrown clear. Where's Michelle?

She had been sitting next to him. He recalled the sound of her laughter and then, moments before the impact, her screams. Anguish gripped his heart like steel talons as he realised she must still be in the car. He strained his eyes, searching for any sign of movement, but the area was obscured by thick black smoke billowing from the burning wreckage. He hoped that Michelle had somehow been thrown clear too, tried not to think of her trapped within the remains of the Lamborghini.

When you stare into the abyss, the abyss stares back at you.

He thought back to how they had met, and their life together. He was a struggling actor, offered a part, his first speaking role, on a television play that she had written. It was a gritty, kitchen-sink drama about a mother forced to take her three young daughters to a hostel to escape an abusive marriage. It highlighted issues not widely discussed in the media at that time and propelled Michelle and him into the limelight.

They hit it off from the outset, and since meeting they had not spent more than one day apart. They were married six months later, in a no-frills ceremony at a Registry Office in Brighton, after which they went for fish and chips on the beach. In addition to exchanging rings, they bought one another Rolex wristwatches, Michelle certain that they would be good investments for the future. Unlike many showbusiness marriages of convenience, Simon and Michelle lived for one another and recently had been trying for a baby.

Thanks to her, Simon landed further TV roles and then crossed over into films, his latest being a part alongside Michael Caine in 'The Italian Job', that earned him very favourable reviews and an offer to work in Hollywood. The film also gave him the desire to emulate the opening scene by driving an orange Lamborghini Muira through the Alps.

Simon found a secondhand Muira at a dealership in London. It was a P400 in orange, and for the full 'Italian Job experience', he fitted a radiocassette player and bought a tape of Matt Monro that included the song, 'On Days Like These.'

The trip was meant to be their holiday before they both flew out to LA. Deep down, Simon knew that Michelle would have preferred a different kind of break to being cooped up in a noisy, uncomfortable sports car and thrown around the twisting switchbacks of a notorious Alpine road, and yet she smiled without complaint and said she was looking forward to it.

Simon had also been warned by fellow enthusiasts about the tendency for carburettors to leak fuel onto the engine, causing Muiras to catch fire – a fact he had neglected to mention to Michelle. Now, it seemed, his chickens had come home to roost.

He contemplated scrambling down the ravine and searching for Michelle. Ordinarily he would have done so without even thinking about it, but he found that a kind of inertia had befallen him, stripping him of any desire to move from the edge of the road. Instead, he continued staring at the carnage below, hoping against hope that Michelle would appear, look up and wave to him that everything was alright.

Simon shivered as a chill passed through him. *Someone walking over your grave.*

Before the crash, it had been like they were driving beneath an upended bowl painted in brilliant cobalt. Now the sky was grey, not misty or cloudy, just grey. As if its colour had somehow drained away.

He shivered again as the air grew colder still. Frowning as he sought to make sense of what was happening. Down in the ravine the Muira had burned itself out. The smoke was almost gone, revealing the true extent of the damage. The car was on its roof. It must have rolled end-over-end because its front and rear were concertina'd into a twisted mess almost a third of the original length of the car.

As he stared, Simon began to make out more detail. Stubs of scorched plants lined the gaps between smoke-blackened rocks. Automotive debris surrounded the wreckage; pools of melted rubber; shards of plastic and windscreen glass scattered around like spilled diamonds.

And then somehow he was inside the Muira. The interior had been incinerated. Everything flammable was gone. Instruments and switches dangled by strands of copper from the ruined dashboard, like a mobile above a child's bed. The seatbelts must have burned through because the bodies lay slumped at the bottom of the wreckage, flesh roasted to a crisp, teeth bared in rictus grins that seemed too large for their blackened, shrunken heads. They had been holding hands, her left in his right, the steel band of the Rolex still visible on her wrist.

As realisation dawned, Simon looked up at a familiar sound.

The Lamborghini Muira emerged from the tunnel and slowed to a halt. As Simon stood up the driver's door opened, Matt Monro singing softly in Italian.

The driver's seat was empty.

Michelle smiled from the passenger seat, her hand resting on the swell of her midriff.

"It's time to go, Simon," she said.

Journeyman Blues

Written for my friend, Steve Chilvers.

Mine is a story

of heartache and shame

Of drink-sodden nightmares

And living with pain

I would've crawled down to hell

For a bottle of Jack

Now I'm walking the line

And I ain't going back

See, I found my way forward

And I set myself free

I've locked up my demons

And swallowed the key

The path wasn't easy

I had stones in my shoes

I tripped and I stumbled

Gave in to the booze

My life was a spiral

Of blackouts and bars

But as I lay in the gutter

I looked at the stars

Then along came a woman

Who loved me for me

We leaned on each other

To set ourselves free

Now I'm using my hands

and I'm using my brain

I find my salvation

When I go with the grain

I give thanks for my mojo

My soulmate, my muse

And I'm living my life

And I'm making the blues

Beelzebub Jones Trilogy

The following three stories came about when Hull musician, Andrew McLatchie, posted on Facebook that he'd had an idea for a one-off concept album with a supernatural, spaghetti-western theme.

When I offered to write a short story to accompany it, Andrew sent me a brief plot synopsis, together with a demo of the opening track. As soon as the demo started to play, the opening scene appeared in my head, I began writing and what you are about to read is pretty much the story as it unfolded. What began as a one-off project grew into a trilogy. Working with Andrew, has been an absolute pleasure and this project has been one of the most creatively rewarding things I've ever taken on.

A Good Day to be a Bad Guy

Sunup

Sunrise painted the canyon with colours to match the glowing embers of the dying camp fire.

Beelzebub Jones sipped whisky from a battered tin mug as he stared at the distant town.

Half a mile away, and about a hundred feet in the air, a group of vultures turned lazy circles, waiting patiently for something, or someone to turn to carrion.

Scavengers of the fallen.

Takers of the dead.

Vultures bothered him, always had, in a preternatural way that he couldn't define. Like a vague memory from a previous life, or maybe a premonition of things to come.

If he believed in such things.

Turning his gaze back to the town, he swallowed the last of the whisky, tossed the mug to one side, shucked the coarse blanket from his shoulders, and cast a long shadow as he stood up and unbuttoned his pants.

The campfire hissed its death throes, throwing up clouds of ammonia-scented steam as the torrent of piss deluged the hot ashes.

Shaking off the last drops, he buttoned up, picked up his battered Stetson, and then pulled two Colt .45 Peacemakers from the holsters slung low over his hips.

Both were fully loaded. Twelve rounds, ready to go.

Replacing the pistols, he took a cheroot from the pocket of his leather jerkin, lit, inhaled, and stared once more across the desert landscape.

After a few moments of reflective smoking, he turned towards a tall Sequaro, where a piebald mustang stood motionless, loosely hitched to the giant cactus by a single leather rein. He strode towards it, pulled a Winchester rifle from the saddle holster and ejected six shells.

That would have to do.

He reloaded, pulled a canvas sack from a saddlebag, placed the rifle inside, pulled the drawstring together and slid the sack back into the holster.

Next, he unfastened the saddle bags and tossed them to the ground. He needed to travel light, and come sundown he planned to be safely over the border, and a very rich man.

The mustang snorted as, in a single movement, Beelzebub Jones snugged the reins, grabbed a fistful of mane, put his left foot in the stirrup, and swung himself onto the saddle.

His head full of trouble, dark thoughts clouded his mind as Beelzebub Jones adjusted his Stetson, wheeled the mustang around and headed towards the town.

Soon the vultures would have new meat to feed on.

Today was going to be a good day.

The Heist

He rode into the shimmering town just before noon. The merciless heat had driven most folks indoors, save for a couple of old timers in rocking chairs in the scant shade of the porch outside the General Store. They stared in silence as the tall stranger dismounted and lead the mustang to a water trough.

While the horse drank, Beelzebub Jones filled his canteen as he surveyed the town. He took a few moments to formulate a plan, and then walked the mustang to a hitching post outside a down-at-heel saloon.

Conversation stopped as he walked inside. Behind the counter, a greasy-haired bartender with a doleful moustache and powerful body odour, wiped dirty glasses with a grubby towel.

"Howdy," said the bartender. "Sure is a hot one today."

Beelzebub Jones walked up and placed a silver dollar on the scarred wooden bar-top.

"How much whisky will that get me?"

The bartender sniffed. "Two half-pints."

"Open one now, I'll take the other with me."

The bartender nodded, and slid two bottles and a shot glass across the bar. "You ain't from round here," he said.

Beelzebub Jones swallowed a shot of whisky. "I guess not."

"You stoppin' here," said the bartender. "Or just passin' through?"

Beelzebub Jones took another shot. "Well," he said. "Since you ask, I'm fixin' to rob the bank, maybe shoot someone too. I ain't quite worked out the details yet."

He filled and then emptied another glass.

"You see," he said. "It's been awhile since I shot anyone, and every now and then I gets me a hankering to do it again."

The bartender stared at him. "You sure got a strange sense of humor, mister."

"Yeah, I hear that a lot."

Beelzebub Jones drained the last of the whisky, placed the second bottle in the pocket of his jerkin, and then tipped his Stetson at the bartender.

"Nice talking to you," he said, and then turned and walked out of the saloon.

Outside, he led the mustang across the street, and hitched the reins to a post next to the bank.

Beelzebub Jones took a last look around, pulled the canvas sack from the saddle holster, untied the drawstring, withdrew the Winchester, and walked into the bank.

The metallic double-click got everyone's attention.

Three customers, standing in line, turned and gasped as Beelzebub Jones levelled the rifle.

"This here's a robbery," he drawled. "You folks git on the floor an' you won't get hurt. Do it NOW!"

All three customers lay down without a word.

"That's good," he said. "Stay right there."

The manager and a teller stood behind the counter.

Beelzebub Jones threw the canvas sack to the manager, and then shouldered the Winchester.

"Fill that up," he said. "Nice and quick, and don't try nothin'."

"Mister," said the manager. "Last feller tried to rob this bank is still hanging outside the courthouse. You won't get to the end of the street."

Beelzebub Jones blinked once, and shifted the gun barrel to the right. Customers screamed at the explosion, the manager yelped as the teller's brains spattered his face.

Beelzebub Jones aimed the Winchester at the manager. "Now I tried askin' nice," he said. "You don't fill that sack right now, I'ma shoot someone else, and then I'ma shoot you."

The manager whimpered, his hands shaking as he opened drawers, quickly filled the sack with cash, and placed it on the counter.

"Now, that wasn't so hard, was it?" Beelzebub Jones grabbed the sack and nodded towards the crumpled body of the teller.

"My condolences for your loss," he winked.

The Getaway

Beelzebub Jones walked calmly out of the bank, waved to the crowd that had gathered, mounted the mustang and was halfway along Main Street when he heard the first gunshot and sound of hoof-beats behind him.

"Well hell, that didn't take long."

The posse were closing fast.

"C'mon, boy, time to show 'em what you got." Beelzebub Jones tapped the horse's flanks and leaned forwards as the powerful mustang surged into full gallop, opening the distance from the posse as they headed out of town. After half a mile, Beelzebub Jones looked back. The posse were still some distance back, but starting to gain ground. Soon they would be close enough to start shooting. He had to get off the trail.

He steered the mustang onto rough ground, the nimble horse instinctively finding the best route as they raced towards a group of boulders at the base of a mesa.

As soon as they were safe behind cover, Beelzebub Jones grabbed the Winchester, dismounted and slapped the mustang on the rump. As it cantered away he clambered up the boulders, finding a vantage point about twenty feet up.

He got into firing position just as the six-man posse came into view, took a bead on the closest rider, held his breath and exhaled softly as he squeezed the trigger.

A red rose appeared on the rider's chest, blood flying from his back as he fell sideways, his body bouncing as the horse dragged him at full gallop for several yards before his foot dislodged from the stirrups.

Beelzebub Jones dropped four more riders, leaving only the sheriff.

"Say goodbye, you sonofabitch."

He took aim, squeezed the trigger.

CLICK.

"Goddam it!"

Beelzebub Jones ducked back beneath the lip of the boulder, threw the Winchester to one side, drew a Colt .45, and waited.

After an eternity, he braved a glance. No sign of the sheriff.

He waited some more.

The desert was silent save for the call of a golden eagle high overhead. Cautiously, Beelzebub Jones began to descend, measuring each step, careful not to dislodge any stones, or to make any sound.

The first bullet ricocheted off the boulder, an inch from his head. As he dived for cover a second bullet hit him in the left shoulder.

Frantically, Beelzebub Jones scrambled around the boulder, fumbled the whisky bottle out of his pocket, pulled the cork out with his teeth and took a long drink as he took stock.

Somewhere behind him was the sheriff. In front and to his left lay open desert. His only chance for cover was a pile of rocks, fifty yards to his right.

Fifty yards of open ground, with a bullet in his shoulder.

Slowly, he pushed himself to his feet, the exertion sending fresh waves of agony down his arm. As he waited for his head to clear, he smiled as something beyond the boulders caught his eye.

Beelzebub Jones checked the Colt .45, took a step to his right, peered around the boulder, stooped low and sprinted for the rocks.

Halfway across the open ground, he saw the sheriff break cover, levelling his Winchester as he ran towards him. Beelzebub Jones fired three shots, and then crashed to the ground, crying out at the sledgehammer punch to his stomach as the Winchester gunshot echoed around the desert. He lay for a second, blood spilling from his guts, and then lifted his head.

The sheriff took aim again, and then sprinted for cover as Beelzebub Jones fired the Peacemaker three more times, drew the second pistol and crawled towards the rocks.

A bullet careened off the boulder. Beelzebub Jones fired two shots, keeping the sheriff at bay as he staggered towards the far side of the rocks.

"I got me a poster here," The sheriff's voice boomed across the desert. "Got a pitcher of your ugly mug, says 'Wanted, Dead or Alive'." He paused. "Guess which one it's gonna be?"

Beelzebub Jones doubled over, leaning against the rock and gasping in agony as blood poured from his stomach wound.

"Won't be long now," boomed the sheriff. "I seen the shit fly right outta you. Ain't nothin' worse 'n bein' gutshot. You die real slow and it hurts like a sumbitch, so they say."

Beelzebub Jones watched his blood pooling around his boots, felt his breath rattling in his lungs, and coughed again as he tried to whistle.

"That teller you shot, he's mah nephew. I'm a takin' you in if it's the last thing I do. It won't be the first time I strung up a dead man."

Beelzebub Jones hawked, spat a gobbet of thick blood, and whistled again.

The piebald mustang appeared from the far side of the rocks, stepped towards him and stopped next to a small boulder.

"I reckon you must be near 'nuff bled out by now." The sheriff's voice sounded closer. "Make your peace you sumbitch, cos' here I come."

Beelzebub Jones summoned the last of his strength, staggered towards the mustang and somehow clambered onto the saddle and grabbed the reins.

The bullet hit him square in his lower back, the mustang whinnying as the exit wound spattered gore onto its neck.

Drawing his last ounces of willpower, Beelzebub Jones gripped the saddle, turned, raised the Colt .45, and fired. He saw the sheriff's Stetson fly into the air, saw blood spray from the side of his head, saw the sheriff crumple to the ground.

Darkness closed in as he heeled the mustang's flank. He felt the pistol slip from his hand as the horse launched itself towards the desert.

Beelzebub Jones held on at full gallop for about half a mile, his senses shutting down to the blur of the desert, the thunder of hoof beats, and the blood covering the horse's neck.

He didn't feel the mustang stumble, had no recollection of hitting the ground, no sensation of bones shattering.

******

Sometime later his eyes opened wide to dark shapes circling in the sapphire sky.

Scavengers of the fallen.

Takers of the dead.

Beelzebub Jones turned his head. The mustang lay ten feet away in a lake of congealing blood, flies buzzing around the bullet hole in its neck.

He tried to crawl towards it but the pain was too much, and anyway, his legs didn't work.

He felt a tear run down the side of his face, and then heard himself cry out in anguish as a

vulture landed close by, flapped its wings and hop-
skipped towards the dead horse.

Beelzebub Jones looked away, and then
passed out to nightmarish sounds of flesh being
ripped from a still-warm body.

The Crossing Place

He dreamed feverish images of childhood.
Images of a small boy taking the slaps, punches,
kicks and cigar burns from the succession of drunks,
drifters and outlaws that his Momma entertained for
a few dollars, or, more often, bottles of cheap
moonshine.

He saw his Momma on the bed with her
latest man, staring at the ceiling, her skirts rucked up,
the bed thumping against the wall.

Thump.

Thump.

Thump-ump.

Thump-ump.

Thump-ump.

Beelzebub Jones opened his eyes to the
sound of the drumbeat, and the earthen smell of
dried leaves that covered his bare midriff.

He was lying on top of a simple bed fashioned from branches and buffalo hide, inside a large Tipi. Arcane symbols and naïve artwork had been daubed on the animal-skin hides that rippled in the slight desert breeze. Smoked drifted lazily upwards, drawn towards the hole at the apex of the poles.

Thump-ump.

Thump-ump.

Thump-ump.

Beelzebub Jones twisted to look for the drummer, and then gasped as a stiletto of pain tore through his stomach.

"Hold on, Cochise." A deep voice boomed around him. "You in a bad way, son. Gonna need time to heal."

"Where am I? Who are you?"

"Time enough for that, son. All in due course."

A pause.

"Seems you've had you quite the day."

Beelzebub Jones twisted his head. "Where are you? I can't see you."

"Shot in the arm," said the voice. "Shot in the guts, front and back. And yet, here we is having us a conversation. Boy, that sheriff's gonna be pissed when he finds out."

"Sheriff's dead," said Beelzebub Jones. "I shot him in the head. I seen him fall."

"Nuh-uh," said the voice. "He still upright. You took his left ear off, but he ain't dead."

"Well now, that is a shame, 'bastard shot my horse."

"That was bad luck," said the voice. "The bullet come outta your guts, went into the mustang's neck. He bled out at full gallop, and yet he still got you outta there. That's gotta be a special kinda horse."

"Best I ever had." Beelzebub Jones tried to look around again. "How do you know all this, anyhow? Where am I?"

A tall, thin man of indeterminate age materialized from the gloom. He wore a dark, threadbare suit and a tall black hat, the shadow of which obscured a gaunt, white-painted face.

"You at the crossing place, son," said The Stranger.

"Am I dead?"

"That's a interesting question. You ain't alive, strictly speaking, but you ain't passed over yet. You're in the shadows where the dead men wait. Ordinarily, folks such as yourself, they passes over with no fuss, no intervention. But you," The Stranger aimed a finger at Beelzebub Jones. "You sir, are an enigma."

"How's that?"

"Raised on hard times and dragged through the dirt. You ain't been dealt the best cards a man can get in his life," The Stranger paused. "You got a stone-cold heart."

"It's the only way to be," said Beelzebub Jones.

"Yeah, but you a special kind o' nasty. You shot that kid in the face from like, two feet away, easy as breathing. You sir, are one mean motherfucker."

"That's my guarantee," said Beelzebub Jones.

The Stranger nodded. "Yes indeed," he said. "And someone like you don't come around too often."

"Someone like me? What's that s'posed to mean?"

"You got a rare talent," said The Stranger. "Be a shame for that to be wasted."

Silently, Beelzebub Jones counted to ten.

"Mister," he said. "You been talkin' in riddles since I woke up. Now I wants you to talk straight, and tell me what in the name of Sam Hill we doin' here inside this Tipi?"

The Stranger stepped towards the table, his eyes glittering as he leaned in close and stroked Beelzebub Jones' face.

"You and me, we're gonna make a deal."

The sound of his voice and the touch of his hand carried the torment of a million souls lost for eternity. Beelzebub Jones shuddered and then moaned, first in terror, and then in shame as he voided his bowels.

"That can happen," chuckled The Stranger. "Jus' means I got your attention."

He stepped backwards.

"How'd you like to walk outta here?" he said. "No more pain, all your wounds healed. Hell, you can even get your damn horse back."

"I'd like that very much," said Beelzebub Jones. "What I gotta do?"

The Stranger disappeared into the gloom and rematerialised carrying a Mason jar of clear liquid.

"Before we goes any further," he said. "All what's gonna happen can only take place with your full agreement. I said I can fix you, an' I can, but it's gonna be on my terms, an' you gotta agree to that before we goes any further."

"What are your terms?" said Beelzebub Jones.

The Stranger's face split into a rictus grin, his eyes twinkling with dark mischief. "Well now, there's the rub," he said. "The only way you gonna find that out is to give me your agreement."

"What if I don't?"

"Well then, you gonna wake up on the desert floor, right where you fell, and you gonna open your eyes an' you gonna see vultures circling. An' then, one by one, you gonna watch 'em drop and hit the dirt, and then the last thing you gonna see is a vulture's head dippin' into yo' guts."

The Stranger paused.

"You got any more questions?"

Beelzebub Jones didn't even blink. "I guess not." he said.

"That's what I thought."

The Stranger dipped two fingers into the Mason jar. Beelzebub Jones flinched as The Stranger painted the liquid onto his forehead.

"All that's yours belong to me," he said. "Fo' now and fo'ever after. Are you in agreement?"

"I am," said Beelzebub Jones.

"And this is yo' own decision, made without coercion or threat?"

"It is," said Beelzebub Jones.

The Stranger dipped his fingers once more into the Mason jar and painted more symbols onto Beelzebub Jones' forehead.

"I'm anointin' you with liquor, in the mark of the single eye and the inverted cross," said The Stranger. "An unholy communion, you might say."

He laid his hand flat on the leaves that covered Beelzebub Jones stomach. Grabbed a handful and squeezed them into pulp

"This gonna hurt," said The Stranger. "Real bad."

He pressed down hard.

Beelzebub Jones screamed as he felt the leaves forced deep into his wounds.

"Ain't nothin' but tobacco," said The Stranger. "Nicotine'll ease the pain, fight off infection."

He pressed harder. A fist of pain hit Beelzebub Jones like a steam train, his scream lifted his shoulders from the bed, and then he passed out.

The Deal is Done

Beelzebub Jones woke to sunlight blowing dust motes through a gap in the Tipi's hide. He looked around, and then down at himself. The leaves were gone, replaced by red welts of scar tissue across his stomach.

"Got yo'self a badge of honour." The Stranger appeared from nowhere. "How you feelin'?"

Beelzebub Jones took a minute to consider this.

"I don't feel no pain, as such," he said. "But I'm somethin' kinda cold inside. Empty, you might say."

"All that's yours belong t'me now," said The Stranger. "That's what I said, and that's how it is."

Beelzebub Jones nodded. "I understand," he said.

The Stranger looked at him. "No son, I don't think you do." He picked up the Mason jar. "Looks like you could use a drink," he said.

Beelzebub Jones sipped, and then gasped as the clear liquid scorched its way down his gullet.

"Tha's moonshine," said The Stranger. "Necessary inebriation. Best there is."

"That's harsh, indeed." Beelzebub Jones grimaced, but took a second drink.

"What happens now?" he said.

"Whatever you want to happen," said The Stranger. "You're free to go your own way, do what you wanna do." He paused. "There's one thing you gotta consider, though."

"Oh?"

"When the moon comes out, there's gonna be a few changes."

"Changes? Like what changes?"

"To your appearance."

"What about my appearance?"

The Stranger shook his head. "It ain't nothin' to worry about, you'll see when it happens."

He paused. "What do you think you're gonna do first?"

Beelzebub Jones thought for a moment. "I wanna go back into town, I gotta score to settle with the sheriff."

The Stranger nodded. "I got you two new pistols," he said. "Colt .45s, just like you had before. I think you'll get along just fine with 'em."

He pointed to some garments folded and stacked on a three-legged stool. "I also got you some new clothes, befittin' of your new status."

"What status is that?"

"Oh, you'll find that out in your own good time."

Beelzebub Jones stood up, walked over to the stool and started to get dressed.

A few minutes later, he pushed the Tipi flap to one side and emerged blinking into the afternoon sun.

'Well now, Mr. Fancy Pants, ain't you the dapper one."

Beelzebub Jones wore a dark suit over a crisp white shirt with a black string tie. A double-holster gun-belt, embroidered with firebird motifs and holding two gleaming revolvers, slung low across his hips.

"I even got you a new hat." The Stranger handed over a black Derby.

Beelzebub Jones raised an eyebrow, then donned and adjusted the hat.

"One more thing you gonna need," The Stranger clicked his fingers. Beelzebub Jones turned to the sound of hoof beats and smiled as the piebald mustang cantered into view.

"That's one feisty damn horse," said The Stranger. "Seemed fittin' that you two be reunited."

Beelzebub Jones held the mustang's bridle, stroking its head as he breathed gently into its nostrils.

"Best damn horse I ever had," he said.

"Well, I think that's our business concluded," said The Stranger. "The deal is done," he grinned. "Live a life devoid of grace, and go forth and sin all you fuckin' want."

His grin stretched wider. "Nicotine, liquor and blasphemy. The unholy trinity. It's all a man needs."

Beelzebub Jones nodded to the Stranger, mounted the Piebald mustang and cantered out into the desert.

The Gunfight

The sun was low in the sky when Beelzebub Jones rode into town. Townsfolk on Main Street stared as he stopped outside the saloon, dismounted, tied the Mustang to the hitching rail and walked through the batwing doors.

The bar fell silent as Beelzebub Jones walked to the counter.

"Thought you was dead," said the barkeeper. "Sheriff said you was gut shot, said the last time he seen you, you was just about bled out, said the vultures was circling."

Beelzebub Jones placed his boot on the brass foot-rail, and slipped the hem of his suit-coat to clear the holster on his right hip, his fingers caressing the handle of the pistol.

He looked around the bar, sniffed and then turned to the barkeeper.

"Looks to me like the sheriff was exaggerating somewhat," he said. "Last time I seen him he's bleeding from the head."

"Well," said the barkeeper. "Whatever happened, you pissed off a lotta folks in this town. The sheriff deputised a whole bunch of mean motherfuckers to replace the posse you kilt. They're all gonna be mighty glad to see you."

Beelzebub Jones' mouth twisted into a terrible smile. "Looks like me and the deputies got us a lot in common."

The barkeeper leaned in close.

"Mister," he whispered. "If I pour you a drink on the house, and give you a half-pint of whisky, what are the chances of you leavin' my saloon and raisin' hell somewhere else?"

The double-click of a Winchester rifle stopped all conversation.

"Beelzebub Jones. Put up your hands you sonofabitch."

Beelzebub Jones turned around slowly.

The batwing doors framed a tall figure, backlit by kerosene lamps that hung from the porch, the stock of the Winchester pressed against his cheek.

"I'm a deputised lawman," he yelled. "Sworn in by the sheriff. Now throw me your gun belt and I'ma walk you outta here, and you're gonna come with me to the jailhouse."

He paused.

"An' I ain't gonna ask you twice, there's five more like me and the sheriff's a-waitin'. You ain't ever gonna leave this town."

Beelzebub Jones inhaled slowly, his nostrils flaring as he stared at the lawman. He held his breath for a heartbeat and then breathed out, felt his lips twitching as delicious sensations swirled and shivered through his body.

The lawman sneered. "What're you smilin' at?"

"I was just thinking to myself," said Beelzebub Jones. "This could be a good day."

The Colt .45 appeared in his right hand. He felt the recoil, saw the flame spit from the barrel, heard the lawman scream as the barrel of the Winchester blew apart in his face.

The rifle clattered to the floor as the lawman clutched at his ruined eyes. "I cain't see," he screamed. "I cain't…"

Women screamed as the lawman's head exploded, glasses smashing as his body crumpled onto a table and then rolled onto the floor.

Beelzebub Jones blew smoke from the barrel, plucked two bullets from his gun-belt, reloaded the Colt Peacemaker, stepped over the dead lawman, paused at the batwing doors, and then walked out of the saloon and into the middle of the strcet.

He paused to glance at the fat moon veiled by a large cloud, felt a rush of exhilaration at was to come.

"Well, well, well. If it ain't Mr. Jones."

His back to the saloon, Beelzebub Jones turned to see the sheriff standing twenty yards away to his left, flanked by two deputies.

"Evenin' sheriff," he said. "How's the ear?"

"Laugh while you can, you sum'bitch. Like I said out there in the desert, you're wanted dead or alive. There's only one way this's gonna end, and that's with you in a box."

The sheriff smiled. "But first we're gonna have us some fun. Take a look behind you."

Beelzebub Jones turned to his right to see three lawmen appear from an alley, walk into the street and took up position in line across the street.

He looked back at the sheriff. "You got me covered from both sides," he said. "Six against one. You sure you got enough men?"

"Well sir," said the sheriff. "We could shoot you right now. But I'ma give you a sportin' chance."

He turned and yelled towards the saloon. "Jeb! Get out here."

The barkeeper emerged from the saloon and stepped out onto the boardwalk.

"Be careful, sheriff," he gabbled. "This'n just put a bullet down the barrel of a Winchester. I seen it with my own eyes. Straight down the barrel. The Winchester blew up in Luke's face, right before his head blowed apart. Ain't never seen shootin' like it."

"Is that right?" said the sheriff. "Well then, we should have us a good show."

"What do you want me to do?" Said the barkeeper.

"The sheriff smiled. "I just wants you to count t'three. You think you can do that?"

"Sure," frowned the barkeeper. "I can do that."

"That's all I need to know." The sheriff winked at Beelzebub Jones. "Cos we're gonna have us a good ol' fashioned quick draw."

Beelzebub Jones raised an eyebrow. "You sure you don't wanna deputise a few more lawmen? Just to make it equal?"

"No, I think this'll do just fine."

Beelzebub Jones looked around, and then back at the sheriff. "Where y'all are stood, you better make sure you don't shoot each other."

The sheriff smiled. "Oh don't you worry about that. We got this all planned out. You stand right where you are, and we'll take up our positions."

"Do what you want, sheriff," said Beelzebub Jones. "But this ends today, and whatever happens, you brought it down on yourselves."

"Well, sir," said the sheriff. "We can do it on the count of three, and you gets a chance, or I can shoot you dead right now. 's up to you."

Beelzebub Jones turned to face the saloon, flexed his shoulders and rolled his neck.

"Let's dance," he said.

"You ready, Jeb?" yelled the sheriff.

"I guess," said the barkeeper.

"Well OK, then. Jeb's gonna count, and we're gonna draw on three."

A stiff breeze blew up, rolling the cloud across the sky as it moaned along the street, lifting whorls of sand in brief cones that span and then collapsed.

As Jeb stepped forward, Beelzebub Jones looked sideways to the three lawmen on his left.

Silence rang in his ears and then he heard Jeb take a deep breath.

"ONE."

Beelzebub Jones looked sideways to the sheriff and two deputies.

The cloud drifted on.

Beelzebub Jones gasped as moonlight climbed his body. Felt his face tighten, his blood rush, and his senses heighten to the point of all-knowing.

"TWO."

Beelzebub Jones stared up at the glowing moon, and understood. He inhaled deeply, exhaled slowly and lifted his head. Once again he felt the smile play around his lips.

This will be a good day.

"THREE."

Beelzebub Jones felt his body lift, became cruciform, head tilted upwards, laughing at the sky as five lawmen to his left and right fell simultaneously beneath a fusillade from his Colt .45s.

The sheriff yelped as both guns were shot from his hands, and then screamed in horror. He turned to run, tripped and sprawled headlong.

Beelzebub Jones blew smoke from his gun barrels as the sheriff looked back at him, his face twisted in terror.

"What. What are you?"

"Why sheriff, whatever is the matter?"

"Your, your face…"

Beelzebub Jones grinned, and then laughed maniacally as he raised his hands to the sky.

"I have been baptised," he yelled. "I am born again, this poor sinner has become a disciple of the night."

He stepped towards the horse trough, and then stifled a gasp at the sight of the skeletal face dancing in the water beneath the vast shimmering full-moon halo. He saw the face of death peel into a fiendish grin, and then look down at the bony claws still gripping the two Colt .45s.

Beelzebub Jones looked up. Jeb the bartender had fled, the street lay in moonlit silence save for the whimpering of the sheriff.

"Broke my ankle," he gasped. "I cain't get up."

Beelzebub Jones levelled his right arm, the Colt revolver steady like an accusing finger as he pulled back the hammer.

"You lose, sheriff," he said.

The sheriff sat up, mustering the final dregs of bravery.

"Well, hell," he spat. "Go on and shoot me if you're gonna. But know this, by shooting deputised lawmen, the bounty on your head just tripled. Killin' a sheriff gonna double that again. There ain't nowhere you gonna be able to stay for more than a couple of days before some low-down, rat-bastard snake recognises you from the wanted posters that are gonna be stuck on every building from here to Frisco."

Beelzebub Jones smiled. "Your deputised lawmen, they died fair and square in a gunfight that started out as six on one."

He paused. "And I got me a saloon fulla' witnesses to you organising it."

Beelzebub Jones shrugged. "As for bein' on wanted posters, I'm kinda used to that. It's who I am, it's who I'll always be."

Three seconds later, Beelzebub Jones blew smoke from both revolvers, span them around, slid them back into their holsters, and stared down at the sheriff's dead body.

"And that's for shootin' my horse," he said.

Beelzebub Jones untied the Mustang and rode along Main Street. Out in the desert, he patted the horse's neck, spurred its flanks and galloped towards the moon.

Today was a very good day.

The Forsaken Territory

Beelzebub's Vision

Ten years later…

Stars twinkled like fragments of broken glass on black velvet as Beelzebub Jones stared through whisky-dulled eyes at camp fire flame-demons vanishing into the Badlands sky.

A lonesome coyote howl echoed around the canyon. Beelzebub Jones blinked slowly, grunted and reached again for the stone jug. As the last drops of harsh liquor splashed into his mouth, the jug fell from his hand and he collapsed sideways and began to snore.

Next morning, wisps of tired smoke were all that remained of the fire, and as Beelzebub Jones groaned and dragged himself upright he relived the dream-vision that had invaded his stupor.

His fingers rasped over chin stubble as he stared into the middle-distance and recalled the vivid, complex and glorious images of horror, destruction and wanton savagery that had filled his consciousness with screams of torment.

Thrilled beyond measure, he knew that his apocalyptic vision of annihilation was no mere whisky-induced hallucination. This was a portent of things to come, a prophecy of ultimate obliteration at which he would be at the forefront.

"About damn time," he growled to no one. "Things've been too quiet lately."

As he replayed the images he recalled a figure, a vague, featureless, charcoal sketch representation dancing around the periphery with stiff-legged, spastic movements as he incanted the message.

The message.

Beelzebub Jones frowned. What was the message?

Inhaling deeply, he closed his eyes and drifted back into the dream state, waiting patiently until the figure wisped once more into his periphery.

"Chapel of Bones," it whispered. "Your destiny lies in the Chapel of Bones."

The mustang's snort brought him back to reality. Beelzebub Jones smiled. Next to the campfire lay his battered leather saddle. Unhooking the water canteen from the pommel, he retrieved his Stetson from the desert floor.

Once a striking piebald, thousands of moonlit transformations had faded the mustang's distinctive black and white markings to a ghost-like paleness. The horse slurped noisily as Beelzebub Jones, still reliving fragments of his vision, stroked its mane, his fingers caressing the pock-marked scar at the base of its neck.

The Stetson flew from Beelzebub Jones' hand as the mustang jerked its muzzle and stamped its hoof.

"Ornery ol' bastard, ain't ya?" he growled. "But you're still the best damn horse I ever had."

Minutes later they were good to go. Beelzebub Jones cinched the girth strap, took a final look around the campsite, steadied the mustang and then swung himself onto the saddle.

The only way out of the Badlands was to head east through Redemption Valley. The closest thing to civilisation was a town called Trinity, about four hours away. He figured that was as good a place to start as anywhere.

It was good to have a plan.

Beelzebub Jones adjusted his Stetson, guided the mustang around to point its head eastwards, and then spurred its flanks.

The Preacher

The Church of St. Barnabus was a broken-down wooden building about a mile or so from Trinity. Faded white paint flaked like a skin disease from its rotting structure, and as Beelzebub Jones rode near, the cross at the top of the sagging spire canted over to the left, and slid down the wooden shingles to land upside-down next to an ancient, wind-scored tombstone.

"That happens a lot," he said.

Beelzebub Jones dismounted and tied the mustang to a fence post. Instinctively, his right hand moved to his gun belt, his thumb hooking over the handle of the Colt .45 as he stepped cautiously towards the half-opened church door and then paused in the doorway, waiting for his eyes to adjust from the bleaching sunlight to the darkness of the interior.

"I heard ye' coming along the road," slurred an Irish voice. "Ye may as well come on inside."

Beelzebub Jones pushed open the church door. Sunlight washed in to reveal six rows of pews, separated by a narrow aisle leading to the altar, against which a grizzled old man in ragged priests' vestments lay slumped, necking from a bottle of cheap whisky. The priest frowned as he focussed, and then raised the bottle in salute.

"If Communion wine is the blood of Christ, then American whisky is the piss of Satan. But sure, beggars can't be choosers." He drained the bottle, and allowed it to slip from his fingers, watching intently as it rolled across the wooden floor.

"Don't suppose ye' have any more about ya?" he slurred.

Beelzebub Jones shook his head. "I'm looking for the Chapel of Bones," he said. "I figured a preacher might know where that is."

The priest sat up. His vague, rheumy eyes suddenly alive with recognition. "I know your face," he said. "I've seen it on Wanted posters. You and your kind go around killing anyone who gets in your way, and spreading fear into the hearts of decent, hard-working people."

Beelzebub Jones raised an eyebrow. "I could say the same about your church," he said. "But I ain't here to bandy words."

The priest's face shifted to an expression of low animal cunning. "The Chapel of Bones, ye say? I might have heard of that, but my memory's not what it was. Maybe some money for a little drink might help bring it back?"

The metallic click echoed around the church. The Colt .45, unwavering in Beelzebub Jones' right hand, aimed at the priest's face.

"In my experience, the option of not having a bullet between the eyes has the same effect."

The priest chuckled as he waved a dismissive hand. "Ye think you're the first eejit ever to point a gun at me? Shoot me if you will, I'll go to a better place, and you still won't know. Ye'll find that a bottle, or some coin will be far more persuasive."

"Chapel of Bones, preacher, tell me what you know or I'll walk outta here and leave you bleeding where you lay."

The priest shrugged. And then cleared his throat in a too-loud stage cough, his eyes darting to his left.

Beelzebub Jones' knuckle whitened against the trigger. And then relaxed. "What was that?"

"What was what?" said the priest.

"The noise you tried to cover up. You're hidin' something. Your face looks guiltier than I am."

"I'm hidin' nothin'," said the priest. "This place is full of holes, you heard the wind tryin' to get in, that's all."

Beelzebub Jones looked to the right. Saw the ringbolt in the floor. Saw the outline of the trapdoor. Heard a faint scuffle.

"What's under there?" he said.

The priest shrugged. "A few auld prayer books and bibles. Sure, ye probably heard a rat down there." He paused. "Or a rattlesnake."

His attempt at a grin sealed his fate.

The boom of the Colt .45 mixed with the scream of the priest as the bullet blew his knee apart.

Beelzebub Jones grinned. "Don't want you running off now."

His boots clumped on the wooden floor as he stepped over to the trapdoor. "What's under here, preacher?" he said. "What am I gonna find when I open this up?"

The priest could only moan as he gripped his wounded leg.

Beelzebub Jones cocked his Colt .45, stooped, grasped the ringbolt, lifted the trapdoor and stepped back.

In the void beneath the floor, two small children, a boy and a girl, looked up terrified, blinking at the sudden light, their olive complexions grimy and tear-streaked.

A thousand nightmare images erupted like a cloud of disturbed bats from the subterranean cave of Beelzebub Jones' memory. He looked across to the priest and then back to the children. Kneeling down, he lifted them from the void, his body quivering with rage as he laid them gently on the floor.

"¿Eres mexicano?" he said.

The little girl sniffed, her eyes wary. "Si, senor," she whispered.

"¿Habla usted Inglés?"

She shook her head. "No senor."

"¿estás herido?"

Again, she shook her head. "Estoy bien, pero mi hermano está herido. El cura es un hombre malo."

Beelzebub Jones nodded, and then pointed to the door. "Te mantendré a salvo. Ve afuera y espérame. Mi caballo necesita caricias."

The little girl nodded, took her brother's hand and led him out of the chapel.

When they'd gone, Beelzebub Jones turned to the priest. "I heard tell of some Texas

Rangers who went bad," he said. "Heard they liked to ride across the border, kidnapping women and children and bringing them back to sell to anyone with a proclivity for lascivious tendencies."

He knelt down next to the priest. "That little girl, she told me her brother was hurt. She said that you were a bad man. What did you do?"

The priest screamed as Beelzebub Jones pushed the Colt's gun barrel into his damaged knee.

"It was God's will," gasped the priest. "It meant nothing to them, they're just ignorant savages."

Beezlebub Jones pointed the Colt .45 at the priest's face.

"Pray hard, preacher. Your time is over."

"You're the devil himself," spat the priest.

Beelzebub Jones grinned. "No, no I ain't," he said. "But I've been drunk with him, and I've pissed on hell-fire."

And then he shot the priest in the face.

Outside, the children stood in shadow of the mustang.

Beelzebub Jones squatted in front of the little girl. "El sacerdote ya no te hará daño," he said. "¿Cuál es tu nombre?"

"Rosalita," she said.

She pointed to her brother. "Su nombre es Jesús."

Beelzebub Jones sighed. "Of course it is."

He stood upright, lifted them both onto the saddle, untied the reins and led the mustang away from the chapel.

"¿A dónde vamos?" said Rosalita.

Beelzebub Jones turned to look at her. "Te llevaré a una ciudad donde estarás a salvo," he said.

"Gracias Señor," she smiled. "Eres un buen hombre."

Beelzebub Jones turned away. "No," he said. "No, I ain't."

Trinity

Two hours later they approached the town of Trinity, the mustang's hooves scuffing up dust clouds along Main Street as curious townsfolk turned to stare.

Beelzebub Jones led the mustang to a water trough outside the General Store. Two elderly women, clad in identical dark, mud-stained prairie dresses and white bonnets watched on with silent disapproval.

As the horse drank, Beelzebub Jones turned and tipped his Stetson to the two women. "Good day, ladies," he said. "Has this town got a doctor? Or a teacher, maybe?"

"We got both," sniffed one. "The teacher is the doctor's wife."

Beelzebub Jones nodded. "Perfect," he said. "And where might I find them at this time of day?"

The other woman pointed along the street. "The doctor's place is next to the sheriff's office. He should be there now."

She nodded to the children, her face sour. "What are they, half-breeds?"

Beelzebub Jones' face hardened, but he said nothing.

When the mustang had drunk its fill, Beelzebub Jones moved to its neck, began to lead it away and then stopped and turned to look at the women.

"Thank you for your help, ladies," he said. "I got one more question, if you don't mind me asking?"

The women looked at one another. "What is it?" said one.

"Well, ma'am, looks to me like you two could be a coupla good-time gals. I was wondering if either of you could recommend a good drinking parlor. Somewhere a man can get outside of some cheap rotgut whisky and raise a ruckus in the company of other unwashed ne'er-do-wells?" Beelzebub Jones winked. "Maybe a place with some sportin' women waiting upstairs to do business on their backs?"

He paused long enough to relish their contemptuous outrage.

"And to answer your earlier question, no ma'am they ain't half-breeds. They're children, and right now there's a priest bein' shown around hell for what he done to them."

Minutes later he tied the mustang to a hitching post outside the doctor's office and was about to step up onto the porch when the door opened and a tall, well-dressed man stepped outside.

"Can I help you?"

Beelzebub Jones nodded. "I'm looking for the doctor."

"You found him."

"I got two kids here, been kinda mistreated. I need you to look after 'em."

"I see," the doctor stared hard. "An' exactly who done the mistreatin'?"

"A certain priest who ain't around no more."

The doctor nodded. "That don't surprise me none. And I'm guessing you had a hand in helping him on his way?"

Beelzebub Jones shrugged, turned to the mustang, pulled a draw-strung leather pouch from the saddle bag and offered it to the doctor.

"Gold nuggets," he said. "Should be enough to pay for whatever it takes to put 'em right. If it ain't, I'll bring the rest next time I'm in town."

The doctor looked at the children and then back at Beelzebub Jones.

"I guess I can do that," he said. "But I don't want your gold."

Beelzebub Jones frowned.

"How's that?"

"Well," said the doctor. "I ain't one to judge, but I'm guessing that whoever owned that gold before you didn't give it up easy, so I'd rather not have anything to do with it."

He looked back at the children. "I'll take care of 'em," he said. "And when they're healed, my wife'll give 'em some schooling. They'll be safe with us."

He paused. "You got my word on that."

Beelzebub Jones thought about this, and then nodded. "I'll be checking up on 'em next time I'm around," he said. "So I guess we'll see how good your word is."

"I know who you are," said the doctor. "I seen the posters. There's a price on your head in this town, dead or alive."

Beelzebub Jones grinned. "You gonna turn me in, doc?"

The doctor shook his head. "No I ain't. The way I see it, any man who brings two kids to me and offers me gold to look after 'em, well, he can't be all bad."

Beelzebub Jones grunted. "Hold on to that thought," he said.

He lifted the children down onto the porch and then squatted in front of them. "Este es un doctor," he said. "Es un buen hombre, te cuidará. Nadie te va a lastimar más."

The children nodded solemnly as Beelzebub Jones ruffled their hair and then straightened up.

"Say," he said. "You ever heard of the Chapel of Bones?"

The doctor shook his head.

"Can't say I have," he said. "But I ain't been here too long. There's an old timer, name of Gabby, hangs out in the Wormy Dog Saloon. He used to be a prospector, panned for gold from here to Mexico, so they say. Might be worth asking him?"

142

"What's he look like?"

The doctor grunted. "Like someone warmed up a dead skunk. Smells like he wants to be alone and his mouth's all rotten from too much chewin' tobacca."

Beelzebub Jones nodded. "Appreciate that," he said.

"You want me to go and get him?"

Beelzebub Jones frowned. "Why would I want you to do that?"

"Mister," said the doctor. "I recognised you straightaway. Like I said, I ain't gonna be responsible for the hanging of a man who saved the lives of two little 'uns, but there's plenty in this town who'd sell out their own mother for a dollar, and you'll find most of 'em in the Wormy Dog."

He paused. "And likely you won't get no trial. They'll drag you up to Hangman's Hill at sundown."

Beelzebub Jones scratched his chin, and then looked up at the sky.

"Sundown, you say?" he said. "Why's that?"

The doctor shrugged. "That's what the sheriff likes to do. Kind of a tradition. The whole town gathers on Hangman's Hill. Outlaws gets hanged and then everyone gets drunk by torchlight. Why are you smiling?"

"Oh, I was just thinking I might get time for a couple drinks before they put a noose around my neck."

"You got a strange sense of humor, mister."

Beelzebub Joncs nodded. "Yeah, I hear that a lot."

He looked back up at the sky, and then back to the doctor.

"You got a stable around here?"

The doctor frowned. "Sure, it's around the back. Why?"

Beelzebub Jones grabbed the mustang's reins.

"I got a favor to ask," he said.

The Wormy Dog Saloon

Beelzebub Jones could hear the ruckus from down the street. As he approached the Wormy Dog Saloon, the sound of 'Turkey in The Straw', played on an out of tune piano carried above the roar of yelling and fighting.

He reached the bat-wing doors and then stepped aside as a body flew past him, cleared the porch and hit the street in a cloud of dust.

Beelzebub Jones steadied a swinging door, checked the derringer in his pocket and then walked into bedlam. A card game that had degenerated into a free-for-all had drawn a crowd of drunks, all yelling encouragement as fists flew in a whirlwind of teeth and blood.

At the far end of the bar, the piano player hammered the keys of the battered upright as if his life depended on it. Next to him a wet-brained old-timer spat gobs of black liquid with unerring accuracy into a dented spittoon as he lurched around in a semblance of a clog dance, almost in time with the music.

Feeling naked without his gun-belt, Beelzebub Jones skirted the brawl and made his way to the bar.

The bartender had to lean close to be heard, "Howdy," he said. "What can I get you?"

Beelzebub Jones saw the glint of recognition in his eyes.

"Whisky," he said. "Cheapest you got, and keep it coming."

The bartender's hands shook as he poured the whisky into a filthy glass. "You ain't here to cause trouble are you, mister?" he said.

Beelzebub Jones shook his head and lifted his hands. "Ain't wearing my guns. I'm just here for a drink."

He leaned onto the bar, lifted the glass, quaffed the harsh liquor and offered the glass to the bartender.

"Leave the bottle," he said.

The bartender nodded. "You got it."

Beelzebub Jones poured another shot.

"I'm looking for Gabby," he said. "You know where he is?"

The bartender nodded towards the piano. "That's him dancing," he said. "There's a gal he likes upstairs, but he cain't afford her so about this time every day he's drunk enough to make him think that he can dance his way into her bed."

He shook his head.

Beelzebub Jones poured another whisky, and then gestured to the bartender. "You know who I am?" he said.

The bartender nodded, terrified.

"Well, today's your lucky day."

"How's that?" said the bartender.

"Because," said Beelzebub Jones. "I figure somebody's gonna run to the sheriff and claim the reward for me, so it might as well be you."

The bartender frowned. "I ain't sure I understand?"

Beelzebub Jones leaned closer. "I need to speak to Gabby," he said. "If he tells me what I want to know, I'll give you the nod and then you go and get the sheriff."

"If I get the sheriff, you're gonna be hanged tonight."

Beelzebub Jones winked. "You can't kill what will not die," he said. "Get me another glass and I'll have a talk with Gabby."

The bartender shrugged. "You got it."

****

When the song finished, Gabby leaned against the wall and launched a volley of tobacco-juice into the spittoon.

"Are you Gabby?"

He lurched around at the sound of his name, his liquor-sodden eyes struggling to focus.

"Who wantsh t'know?" Stumps of blackened teeth were arranged like broken gravestones in ulcerated gums. Beelzebub Jones winced at the cancerous breath that whistled between them.

"I need some information," he said. "And I been told that you might help me."

Gabby swayed as he considered this.

"Whatsh'innit for me?"

Beelzebub Jones waved the whisky bottle. "I'm looking for the Chapel of Bones," he said. "You know where that is?"

Gabby's eyes narrowed in frontier cunning. "Maybe."

As Beelzebub Jones leaned in close the derringer appeared in his hand. "Don't even think of fucking with me, old timer. If you know where it is you get the whisky. Try and test me one more time and I'll put a bullet in your head."

Gabby blinked slowly at the pistol and then lifted his face.

"Silverton," he said.

"Where's that?"

"'s a ghost town now," said Gabby. "Built around the silver mines. Silver ran out, and then…"

Gabby shrugged and then belched poison gas.

"So, the chapel's in Silverton?" said Beelzebub Jones. "In the ghost town?"

Gabby cackled and shook his head.

"In the sheriff's office," he said.

"What's in the sheriff's office?"

Gabby cackled again.

Beelzebub Jones grabbed his shoulder. "You're not making sense," he said. "I want the Chapel of Bones, not the sheriff's office."

Gabby's eyes focused for a second. "There's a map in the sheriff's office," he said. "Pinned to the wall. I seen the Chapel of Bones marked on it."

"And you're sure about that?"

Gabby shrugged. "I spent a lot of time with the sheriff," he said. "Most nights in a cell til I sobered up. I remember every inch of his office, and I remember the map."

"OK," said Beelzebub Jones. "Is it still there?"

"How the hell do I know?" said Gabby. "I ain't been there since everyone left. That's gotta be..." he frowned at the calculation. "That's gotta be ten years."

Beelzebub Jones nodded and handed over the bottle.

As Gabby suckled like a newborn, Beelzebub Jones returned to the bar and called the bartender over. "You can go and get the sheriff now," he said.

The Arrest

Beelzebub Jones was standing at the bar, leaning over his whisky glass when the sheriff burst into the saloon followed by a posse of ten men who fanned out either side of him.

"Beelzebub Jones," yelled the sheriff. "You're a wanted man in fifteen states. By the powers invested in me as sheriff of Trinity, I hereby arrest you and sentence you to be hanged by your neck at sundown. Do you have anything you want to say?"

Beelzebub Jones, drank the whisky, placed the glass on the counter and turned around.

Ten revolvers cocked at once as the posse drew their weapons. Beelzebub Jones raised his hands.

"Hanged at sundown, you say? Don't I gotta stand in front of a judge first?"

The sheriff shook his head. "You're wanted dead or alive, son," he said. "No need to bother the judge. Hell, I could shoot you down where you stand, step over your body and drink me a beer and afterwards folks would shake my hand."

Beelzebub Jones thought about this. "Sundown it is," he said. "I figure y'all are gonna take me to the jailhouse first, though? Cos I'm a might hungry and even a condemned man gets a final meal."

The sheriff sniffed. "We got leftover pork and beans," he said. "You're welcome to a plate 'afore we string you up."

Beelzebub Jones smiled. "Well, hell," he said. "That ain't the worst last meal I've ever had." He nodded to the posse. "Do you think them fine upstanding fellers would mind puttin' away their irons? As you can see I am unarmed and I present no immediate threat to anyone in my vicinity."

The sheriff produced a pair of handcuffs. "They'll put down their guns when I say so," he said. 'Now turn around and put your hands behind your back."

When the cuffs were locked Beelzebub Jones turned to face the sheriff. "There's a derringer in my pocket," he said. "I'm coming quietly and I ain't gonna cause you no trouble."

One of the posse stepped forward, his pistol aimed at Beelzebub Jones' chest.

"Mister," he said. "You sound pretty sanguine for someone who ain't gonna see another sunrise."

Beelzebub Jones smiled. "Sanguine," he said. "That's exactly how I feel, right now."

The posse man snickered. "Let's see how sanguine you feel at sundown when the noose tightens around your neck and you start dancing in the air."

When the saloon laughter died down Beelzebub Jones smiled and nodded. "You can't kill what will not die." He said.

The posse man frowned. "What the hell does that mean? Is that from the bible?"

Beelzebub Jones winked and fifteen minutes later was sitting on a wooden bench staring through the bars of a cell, lost in his thoughts as he scraped cold pork and beans from a metal plate.

He woke to excited voices inside the jailhouse and the sound of a large crowd gathered outside.

The sheriff appeared holding handcuffs and large set of keys. "Time to go, son," he said. "You got any arrangements you want me to make on your behalf? Anyone you want me to contact?"

Beelzebub Jones shook his head. "No thank you, sheriff. All my affairs were sorted out a long time ago."

The sheriff nodded. "Well then stand up and turn around, and put your hands behind your back."

Outside the jailhouse a horse and open wagon was waiting. Behind the driver stood three of the posse, all of them holding Winchester rifles. All of them staring down at Beelzebub Jones as he was manhandled into the wagon.

"Each one of them is just itching to blow your head off," said the sheriff. "So I trust you ain't gonna cause no problems?"

Beelzebub Jones stood and nodded to the crowd. "And deprive these good folks of their entertainment?" he said. "I promise y'all that I will be the best-behaved corpse ever to dangle from Hangman's Hill."

He fell to the boards as the wagon lurched forward, followed by the townsfolk, some carrying burning torches and food hampers.

As the procession moved along Main St. Beelzebub Jones looked across to see the doctor standing outside his office. As their eyes met, the doctor gave the briefest of nods and then the macabre parade headed silently out of town.

Hangman's Hill

Hangman's Hill was a rocky bluff, some forty feet wide and rising to fifteen feet at its highest point. Cracking the bullwhip to get the horses to traverse the gentle slope, the driver brought the wagon to a halt directly below the noose hanging from the oak gallows.

The sheriff clambered onto the wagon, loosened the slip knot, placed the noose around Beelzebub Jones' neck and pulled it tight. Below them the crowd gathered quietly, staring patiently upwards as the execution ritual unfolded.

The sheriff pulled a key from his pocket, unlocked the handcuffs and then tied Beelzebub Jones' wrists with a length of cord. "Saves me coming back for 'em," he said.

He nodded to the posse, who jumped down from the wagon and took up firing positions, their Winchesters aiming into the wagon.

"Before I pass sentence," he said. "Have you got any last words?"

About a mile away, a dust cloud wisped into the air. Beelzebub Jones stared at it, and then smiled.

He looked at the sheriff and winked. "You can't kill what will not die," he said. "You better get some coffins ready, sheriff."

The crowd shuffled uneasily.

The sun was kissing the horizon when the sheriff patted Beelzebub Jones on the shoulder and then half-turned to the crowd.

"Ladies and gentlemen," he yelled. "We are gathered here to serve justice on an outlaw so incorrigible, so heinous that only a rope around the neck will cure him of his criminality."

The sheriff cleared his throat and puffed out his chest. "Wanted in more counties of more states than any of us can remember. The condemned is found guilty of the crimes of murder, armed robberies of citizens, state banks and post offices, horse-stealing, extortion and passing counterfeit money. Therefore, according to the power invested in me as sheriff of Trinity I hereby sentence you, Beelzebub Jones, also known as the Bastard of the Badlands and any other aliases you may go by, to hang by the neck until you are dead."

The sheriff nodded to the cart driver. "Proceed."

The driver cracked the reins. The cart jolted forward and as Beelzebub Jones' heels dragged along the wooden bed, an expectant murmur rose from the crowd, reaching a crescendo as his body swung clear of the cart, the rope snapped taut and his legs began to jerk.

"Lookit him dance," yelled someone.

"Ain't such a bastard now," yelled another.

"Say hello to Satan you fuckin' heathen."

Beelzebub Jones choked and writhed as the noose bit into his neck. Blackness encroached on his senses, tunneling his vision to a pinpoint of light that grew ever smaller. Voices from the crowd faded away, replaced by the erratic pulse thump-thump-thumping in his ears as he swung helplessly.

Pendulum of death.

Oh moon, come on and save me now.

Thump-thump-thump. Filling his head. Counting down.

Thump-thump-thump.

And then a new sound.

Thud-ud-dud.

Thud-ud-dud.

Thud-ud-dud.

Drawing closer.

Becoming louder.

Thud-ud-dud.

Thud-ud-dud.

And then a demonic whinnying squeal.

Approaching from behind, the mustang hit the crowd at full gallop. Broken bodies flying into

158

the air as 800 pounds of muscle mowed through the screaming townsfolk, bucking and twisting, its hooves flailing as it cleared a path to the gallows.

Beelzebub Jones felt his skin tighten as the welcome moonlight crawled across his body.

Flames burned around his neck and wrists, the stench of burning hemp filling his nostrils as he dropped to the ground. Around him the posse raised their Winchesters and then screeched in writhing agony, as simultaneously they combusted into black flames that reached up into the sky, consuming their bodies into piles of ash.

The crowd scattered, screaming as they trampled over one another to escape the whirlwind thrashing of the mustang.

"Best damn horse I ever had."

Beelzebub Jones whistled the mustang over, retrieved his gun belt from the saddlebag, strapped it around his waist with practised ease and leapt into the saddle.

A Colt .45 appeared in his hand as he whirled the mustang around.

On the back of the cart the sheriff stood open-mouthed.

"Skull face," he gasped.

And then the back of his head exploded in a fountain of blood, brain matter, skull fragments and hair.

Beelzebub Jones blew smoke from the Colt .45, holstered it, looked upwards, and then spurred his horse towards the eastern sky.

Silverton

The mustang flew across the open plains. Snorting with exertion, muscles rippling, hooves raising thunder.

Hunched over its neck, Beelzebub Jones laughed maniacally, his senses heightened by the transformation, his body thrilling to the exhilarating wash of the cold night air.

Half a mile ahead, broken pieces of moonlight danced on water.

He slowed the horse, dismounted and began walking. By the time they reached the river the mustang was breathing normally.

Pausing only to allow the mustang a brief drink and to fill his own water bottle, Beelzebub Jones grabbed the reins and splashed across the shallows. As they emerged onto the far bank he looked up at outline of The Silent Mountains, foreboding in the darkness.

Silverton was another half-mile further on. As they walked along Main Street, tumbleweed scudded out of the darkness. Dead, dry structures, fitting inhabitants of a long-dead, abandoned town.

But not completely abandoned.

As he led the mustang past the skeletons of once-buildings, ghostly whispers breezed towards and around him. Voices of the dead, hissing his name, taunting him in sighs carried on the breeze, growing and diminishing, but building in number until it seemed he was surrounded on a deserted street.

Enhanced by transformation, Beelzebub Jones sensed every presence that whirled and reeled around him. Impenitent sin, violence, debauchery and vice filled his consciousness.

Sodom and Gomorrah of the West.

As these words appeared in his mind, Beelzebub Jones found himself overwhelmed by a presence so dark that a shudder of unfamiliar terror washed through him.

"Ain't no righteous people to be found here," said the presence. "The ungodly have perished. What you see now is the legacy of their wickedness."

The voice paused.

"And now here you are," it said. "King of all you survey. Ain't life grand?"

"Better to be the king of shit," said Beelzebub Jones. "Than the shit of kings." His eyes narrowed. "I know you," he said. "You treated me. In the desert."

"Nicotine, Liquor and Blasphemy," said The Stranger. "Ten years, and you've spread my word with zeal and alacrity. You truly are a disciple."

Beelzebub Jones shuddered again. "What do you want with me now?"

"To show you your destiny. You know where it lies?"

"The Chapel of Bones," said Beelzebub Jones. "That was you, in my vision."

"You will find the map," said The Stranger. "And you will find the Chapel. And in the Chapel you will look into the water. And you will see."

"See what?" said Beelzebub Jones.

But The Stranger had gone.

Beelzebub Jones stood alone in the center of Main Street. The voices, stilled by the presence of The Stranger, returned louder and more chaotic and accompanied by silver-grey translucent spectral forms that swirled and span through the air, changing gradually to becoming vague human forms floating inches above the dusty street.

As he walked amongst them Beelzebub Jones felt the fleeting chill-whisper of their touch, experienced fragments of their memories that appeared and then vanished in a finger-snap.

One such form appeared and drifted towards him. As it grew closer it clarified into a skinny young man with half a face, his finger pointing in shaking accusation. "You shot me," said the figure. "You robbed the bank and you shot me."

Beelzebub Jones remembered, but shrugged. "Should've done what you were told," he said. He carried on walking, leaving the ghost of the bank teller to dissipate in his wake.

More figures appeared, crowding the street with memories. Beelzebub Jones recognising each one, and ignoring them all with equal indifference.

Hundreds of victims. Some walked alone but most collected in groups. Each group the vestiges of a phantom posse gunned down by the holstered revolvers that swayed to the beat of Beelzebub Jones' pace as he strode towards the remains of a wooden building at the far end of the street.

Beelzebub Jones stopped outside the Sheriff's office, tied up the mustang and turned around to see a crowd of spectres standing in silent accusation. Apparitions from his past. Consequences of his upbringing and destined to haunt him for eternity.

Staring at the crowd, he chuckled at their expectation of remorse, spat into the dust and then turned and walked into the building.

Inside the Sheriff's office, fingers of moonlight reached in through splintered gaps to illuminate a curling, yellowing Wanted poster pinned to the wall.

Beelzebub Jones ripped down the poster, sneered at his likeness and then rolled it up tightly.

Delving into his shirt pocket he retrieved a box of Lucifer's matches, opened it and struck a match on his boot, sparks hissing and spitting from the match-head as he set fire to the poster.

Beelzebub Jones made his way through the sheriff's office, following dancing shadows as he waved the makeshift torch along each wall. The flame had burned almost to his knuckles when he discovered the map. Right where Gabby had said it would be.

Tossing the remnants of burning paper to the floor, Beelzebub Jones felt around the edge of the map, smiling as the rusting thumb tacks yielded easily. Holding the map carefully he backed away and then turned and walked out of the building. Behind him, the last lick of flame from the embers of the poster kindled a small pile of termite dust, which flared into a larger flame, which reached across to ignite an empty cigarette pack, which burned fiercely next to an upturned wooden chair. The bone-dry wood caught fire instantly, flames engulfing the chair and rising to snatch greedily at a wooden table.

In minutes, the building was ablaze. Timbers cracking and spitting as the fire grew in ferocity. A gust of wind blew sparks to the old saloon next door, and soon that was burning too.

Outside, Beelzebub Jones read the map by moonlight then rolled it carefully and placed it into a saddlebag. Back in the saddle he tipped his Stetson at what remained of the Sheriff's office, turned the mustang around and walked back along Main Street, opening a path through the spectres like breeze through a morning mist.

Behind him, Silverton burned.

Next morning, Beelzebub Jones had skirted the base of the Silent Mountains and was crossing the Hinterland, and as the rising sun lifted clear of the horizon he felt himself revert to human form. This was the first morning that he'd seen without the effects of a gutful of whisky the night before, and he wasn't sure that he cared for it too much.

He rode on until the southern edge of Lake Mysterious came into view. Steering the mustang towards the river, he dismounted, removed the saddle and bridle and watched as the horse rolled and snickered in the dust and then walked to the water's edge.

Beelzebub Jones gathered wood and as flames licked through the campfire he thought back to Silverton and the way the dry buildings went up like tinder.

"Times like these," he said to the mustang. "It truly is a good day to be a bad guy."

A jug of coffee and several strips of beef jerky later, Beelzebub Jones stood up and looked north-east. In the far distance he could just make out the outline of a series of rock bluffs. According to the map, the Chapel of Bones lay somewhere in those rocks.

The Chapel of Bones

Beelzebub Jones woke two hours later.

At the lake's edge he knelt down and submerged his face, the cold-water shock rinsing away the last vestiges of his nightmare.

The mustang stood patiently as it was bridled and saddled and minutes later they were heading north-east.

It was close to noon when they reached the bluffs. Up close they looked impressive, a collection of huge sandstone rocks grouped close together and towering into the sky.

Beelzebub Jones scoured the bluffs, looking for anything resembling a chapel, but saw nothing but seemingly impenetrable and featureless rock.

It was the mustang that found the route in. Without any command from Beelzebub Jones, the horse turned towards the rockface and skipped through a narrow gap that opened into a stone-strewn path that snaked upwards and around the rocks. Beelzebub Jones gave the mustang the rein, sitting back in the saddle as they made their way upwards.

Further up, as it veered left between two huge rocks, the path steepened. Beelzebub Jones dismounted and led the mustang along the narrow path, it's hoof-clops echoing between the stone faces.

The path zigzagged around the rock formations, taking them higher and higher, the gradient becoming so steep that the mustang could no longer walk, scaling the path instead by using a series of jumps, leaving Beelzebub Jones to scramble breathlessly behind.

The mustang disappeared around yet another rock and the air fell silent. When Beelzebub Jones caught up, the path had flattened and widened. Just ahead, the mustang pawed at the ground, snickering and tossing its head.

Beelzebub Jones looked beyond the horse, to a spot where the path disappeared into the gaping black hole of a cave hewn into the rock face.

A black hole framed by a structure formed from human bones.

"Come on in, time's a'wastin'." The familiar voice boomed from inside the darkness. Beelzebub Jones took a deep breath and then stomped towards the entrance.

The cave opened to reveal a vast, majestic cathedral-like space lit by candlelight flickering from a thousand hollowed-out human skulls.

Pillars created by hundreds of intertwined spinal columns stood ten feet apart and towered fifty feet to the roof of the cavern, forming two lines to create a passageway to a hemispherical bowl twenty feet in diameter and twenty feet deep, hewn from stone, its lip ordained with human ribs, fingers and teeth.

A familiar presence shimmered at Beelzebub Jones' periphery.

"Behold the Chapel of Bones," it said. "Reflections will reveal what is unknown."

Beelzebub Jones frowned. "Do what, now?"

He felt a tug on his soul that filled him with darkness as it guided him inexorably towards the immense bowl.

"Kneel before the Font of Destiny," said The Stranger.

Beelzebub Jones knelt. Saw his reflection staring back from the depths of the still, clear water.

"Ain't revealed nothin' yet," he said.

A human skull appeared from beyond the font, lifted into the air, drifted gently towards them and stopped, revolving slowly, inches above the water, as if suspended by an invisible line.

Beelzebub Jones looked closer. Like every other skull in the chapel the cranium had been sawn off at the forehead, the head fashioned into a crude vessel and filled with a dark liquid. The skull revolved once more and then came to rest. Staring directly at Beelzebub Jones.

For a time, nothing happened. And then the skull began to slowly tip forwards, as if nodding in deference.

Or lowering in prayer.

As it did so, the liquid within began to creep towards the edge, and as it spilled over onto the forehead, Beelzebub Jones saw that the dark liquid shone red in the candlelight.

"Human blood," said The Stranger. "Blood of the long, long dead."

Beelzebub Jones stared in fascination as the blood crawled down the skeletal face, covering the teeth, gathering and collecting at the lower edge of the jaw bone and then dropping into the font in great drops of scarlet.

When the blood hit the water, the surface erupted into a torrid maelstrom of pink liquid that swirled, thrashed and boiled.

When the skull was empty, the font water, now clouded a deep pink, became still.

"Reflections will reveal what is unknown," said The Stranger. "Look closely."

Beelzebub Jones leaned into the font. Watched as the blood dissipated, turning the water clear.

No. Not clear. Beelzebub Jones looked closer. In the depths of the font images began to appear. At first indistinct, but then growing in definition to reveal four figures, each positioned as if at a compass point. Each on horseback.

"The Four Horse riders," said The Stranger.

"Like in the Bible?" said Beelzebub Jones. "I always considered that to be a collection of stories, written by men and designed to frighten the ignorant."

"Most of it was," said The Stranger. "But not this."

"So, Revelations is real?"

"Some of it."

Beelzebub Jones looked closer still into the water, peering at the figures.

"Looking down, I can't make out who's who?" he said.

"Start at the West," said The Stranger.

The image on the left changed position to reveal a Native American woman, a knife in her hand, her face painted in fearsome colors, astride a chestnut mustang.

"War woman," said The Stranger. "She goes by the name of Ghigua."

Beelzebub Jones nodded. "Cherokee," he said. "You want a war, them folks'll bring one right to ya'."

"Look East," said The Stranger.

To the right appeared a tall, slim black woman, clad in colorful robes riding high on a jet-black Friesian horse. In her hand she held a pair of balances.

"Famine,' said The Stranger.

"Don't see too many black gals out ridin'," said Beelzebub Jones. "What's her story?"

"Name's Azmera," said The Stranger. "She was a Maasai princess."

"What's a Maasai?"

"Warriors from East Africa," said The Stranger. "Not many got taken as slaves. But she did. And she gave 'em holy hell for it, too."

Beelzebub Jones nodded in admiration.

"To the south is Conquest," said The Stranger.

Directly below Beelzebub Jones the image clarified to show a second Native American astride a white horse and holding a large bow. His face painted white, mouth covered with a red painted handprint.

"Apache," said Beelzebub Jones. "Looks like Chiricahua. The red handprint means he's killed an enemy in hand to hand combat."

The Stranger said nothing.

Beelzebub Jones paused. "Who's the fourth one?"

"In the words of the fourth beast," said The Stranger. "come and see."

Beelzebub Jones looked to the north, squinted at the emerging figure emerged and then gasped as his likeness materialised.

"Behold, Death," said The Stranger.

Beelzebub Jones shook his head. "I don't understand."

"This is your destiny," said The Stranger. "When the seals are opened, hell will follow with you, and y'all will conquer and kill with the sword and with hunger and with death."

A smile crawled across Beelzebub Jones' face. "And then we get to watch the world burn?"

"Pretty much," said The Stranger.

"Will there be whisky?"

"As much as you want."

Beelzebub Jones nodded slowly, his voice softening. "And all good works will be undone," he said.

He gathered his thoughts. "First man I ever killed was a nasty ol' preacher with wanderin' hands. One day he whupped me one time too many, I stole me a Colt .45, stomped on down to the church house and shot him the head. First time I ever fired a gun. Knocked me on my ass and I thought I'd gone deaf."

He smiled at the recollection. "I left town that very day."

"I know," said The Stranger.

"That ol' bastard taught me about The Book of Revelations," said Beelzebub Jones. "Never thought I'd be taking part in it."

"Oh, I never had any doubt," said The Stranger. "Your whole life has been a preparation for this day."

"What do I have to do?"

"You were baptised in mire," said The Stranger. "The son of dirt. Now you will be baptised in blood."

A pause.

"Kneel at the Font of Destiny."

As Beelzebub Jones dropped to his knees, sensed the shimmer move from his periphery to somewhere behind him.

"Once baptised you will leave this place," said The Stranger. "Leave behind your life and cross over to the Place Between. You will have to search out the Horse Riders and together you will fulfil your destinies as each seal is opened."

Beelzebub Jones felt a pressure on his shoulder blades, and then on the back of his head. Felt himself pushed forward, over the edge of the font until his forehead almost touched the crimson water.

"I baptise you in blood," said The Stranger. "Go forth and take your rightful place."

Beelzebub Jones felt the push, heard underwater sounds as his head was immersed three times.

And then an iron grip guided him backwards.

The Chapel was silent. The Stranger gone.

Beelzebub Jones felt the familiar exhilaration as he changed to skeletal form, blood-water dripping from his face as he stood upright.

He grinned as the cavern began to tremble. A low hum building from somewhere, rising to a thunderous roar as the vibrations intensified to juddering tremors. Skulls, loosened by the tremors, dropped to the ground, dust falling from the ceiling as bone structures began to quake and crumble.

Beelzebub Jones stood tall, laughing as the great pillars collapsed around him. Bones splashed into the Font of Destiny, igniting the red liquid into an eruption of oily black flames, instantly filling the cavern with the heat of a thousand hells and devouring everything that was flammable.

As the font roared like a furnace, bones crackled as they blackened and then blazed away to nothing, the intense heat stirring up a blizzard of ash and bone fragments.

It became impossible to breathe. The entrance to the cavern howling as the inferno sucked in a tornado of air, fuelling the fires, transforming the chapel into an incinerator.

And in the midst of it all stood Beelzebub Jones. Cruciform, laughing like a lunatic as the flames swirled around him.

The Doomsday Desperado

The Beginning of The End

Beelzebub Jones sat cross-legged on the desert floor; head bowed, shoulders stooped, his still form painted in the blood of the dying sun.

He looked up at the sound of hoofbeats, saw three riders approaching.

A Cherokee, her face painted in fearsome colors, astride a chestnut mustang. A Maasai Princess, clad in colorful robes riding high on a jet-black Friesian. And an Apache, his face painted white, mouth covered with a red painted handprint that matched the design on the flank of his white Appaloosa.

Beelzebub Jones rose to stand before them.

The three riders reined in their mounts, nodded to him and then spoke as one, each in their own tongue.

Beelzebub Jones heard three words: "We will come."

The riders nodded once more, wheeled their horses and galloped towards the bleeding, shimmering horizon.

Beelzebub Jones stared after them, remaining motionless long after they had disappeared from sight.

"War, Famine and Conquest," said a voice from his periphery. "The Apocalypse Riders."

He looked around, and when he saw that he was alone in the stark, desolate landscape he sank once more to sit cross-legged on the ground, his thoughts melting away, leaving only the ringing silence of the desert stillness.

The mustang's low, throaty whicker woke Beelzebub Jones from the vision. He sat up, his .45 in his hand, eyes fixed on the entrance to the Chapel of Bones. He saw the flicker of a shadow, heard the rattle of a stone, and pulled back the hammer on his revolver.

"Take one more step and it'll be the last one you make."

"I ain't here for trouble, mister."

The voice sounded familiar, and close. Beelzebub Jones rose silently to his feet and moved to take cover behind a large rock just inside the cave.

"Who are you?"

"I'm the doctor from Trinity," said the voice. "I just wanna talk."

"You wearing a gunbelt?"

"I got a Derringer in my coat pocket."

"Toss it where I can see it. Along with your boots."

"My what?"

"Your boots," said Beelzebub Jones. "Take them off and throw 'em where I can see 'em."

A pause.

Beelzebub Jones cocked his other revolver. "Do it now, or I'ma come out shooting."

A Derringer pistol clattered onto the stones outside the cave entrance, followed by two scuffed leather boots.

"Now walk towards me, real slow, hands in the air."

As the figure hobbled into view, Beelzebub Jones holstered one of the .45s; the other remained unwavering in his right hand.

"Stop right there."

"Like I said, I ain't here for trouble," said the doctor. "You can put your gun away."

"I'll decide that. What are you here for?"

"Last time I seen you, you brought in two Mexican kids you rescued from the priest you shot. Then you stabled your horse with me and I let it go when the sheriff took you to Hangman's Hill. Just like you told me."

"I remember," said Beelzebub Jones. "So what?"

"I got a message from the new sheriff."

"What's he want?"

"He wants you. Wants to meet up and discuss your terms of surrender."

"My what?"

"His words," said the doctor. "Not mine. Can I put my hands down, mister?"

Beelzebub Jones holstered the .45 and stepped out of the cave. "Why would the sheriff send the town doctor to parlay with me?"

"He's got the two Mexican kids. Told me to tell you, if you want to see them alive you gotta give yourself up."

Beelzebub Jones' right hand hovered over the .45. "And how did the new sheriff know I had anything to do with those kids?"

"You remember talking to a couple of women in the street? One of them was the sister of the old sheriff. It was her idea to use the kids."

He shook his head. "The new sheriff is one mean hombre, and he's got a stick up his ass about bringing you in. When you killed all them folks on Hangman's Hill they increased the bounty on your head to five thousand dollars, dead or alive."

The doctor sighed. "He wants you real bad, and if he has to kill two Mexican kids he'll find a way of putting that on you."

His paused, his voice shaky. "That ain't all."

Beelzebub Jones frowned. "What do you mean?"

The doctor took a breath before answering. "The Sheriff's raised a posse of outlaws. He told me to tell you that if you don't meet up, they're gonna come after you. And when they catch you they're gonna make you watch while they pass the girl around."

Beelzebub Jones stared hard. "You tellin' me the truth?"

"You got my word, mister. I know who you are. I know what you can do."

"How'd you know where to find me?"

The doctor shrugged. "I been in Trinity a long time, I know perty much all the ranches and homesteads around here, and how to get to 'em. A Navajo ranch-hand told me about the Chapel of Bones. I guessed it was around here, somewhere. And then there was what happened that night."

Beelzebub Jones frowned. "What happened on what night?"

"The night of the storm," said the doctor. "We heard it over in Trinity. There was thunder, lightnin', strange lights in the sky and sounds like the devil was tryin' to dig himself outta hell."

He paused. "I figured you mighta had something to do with that."

"You tell anyone else what you figured?"

The doctor shook his head. "No sir."

"Then why did the sheriff think you'd know where to find me?"

The doctor grunted. "The dead sheriff's sister told him I knew my way around, so the sheriff sent me on my way. He's holdin' them two kids as insurance. Told me to tell you to ride into town and give yourself up. Once you're in jail he's gonna give the kids to me."

Beelzebub Jones stared across the desert; stayed silent for a long time and then turned to the doctor.

"How'd you like to split five thousand dollars?" he said.

The doctor considered this. "Does that mean I can put my boots back on?"

Next morning, the doctor watched as Beelzebub Jones cleaned and loaded his .45s, oiled the holsters on his gun belt, checked his Winchester and loaded a large leather satchel with speed-loaders and shells.

"I'm feeling kinda underdressed," he said.

"Better to have it and not need it," said Beelzebub Jones. "Than need it and not have it."

A battered leather saddle lay astride a wooden sawhorse. Beelzebub Jones hefted onto his shoulder, and then picked up the satchel and the Winchester.

"Let's go pay a visit to the sheriff," he said.

The Ambush

The mustang appeared at the bottom of the mountain track, its once dappled hide bleached pale white by the light of a thousand moons. It pawed the ground, whickering softly as Beelzebub Jones approached.

"That's some horse," said the doctor.

Beelzebub Jones nodded. "Best one I ever had."

A chestnut pony stepped towards the doctor, dipping its head as he grabbed the reins, placed his boot in the stirrups and mounted.

Minutes later, the mustang saddled, Beelzebub Jones swung onto its back, adjusted his Stetson and nodded to the doctor. "Follow me," he said.

An hour later, the mountain trail descended to the desert floor. A mile ahead a range of hills stretched across the horizon.

"We're going over Locust Ridge?" said the doctor.

"Quickest way to Trinity," said Beelzebub Jones. 'Over the top, cross the river and head across the plains. That OK with you?"

The doctor sniffed. "It's a bitch of climb on this side."

"The horses'll be OK. Once we're down the other side, we'll rest by the river for a spell."

They rode on in silence until the ridge loomed over them. Soon, the terrain began to rise, the horses snorting with exertion as they scrabbled up the rocky trail.

As they neared the top, the path flattened and turned to the right, weaving its way between rock formations scattered along the ridge.

As they crested the ridge, the doctor's head erupted in a fountain of blood as a gunshot echoed across the desert.

Beelzebub Jones grabbed the Winchester and leapt from the saddle. A slap to the mustang's rump sent it galloping back down the trail as Beelzebub Jones dived for cover behind a boulder. A second gunshot dropped the doctor's pony, followed by a murderous volley of rifle fire that filled the air with the crack of passing bullets and the spang of lead against rock.

Pinned down, Beelzebub Jones lay prone, showered with stone fragments and dirt as bullets splintered the boulder and tore up the ground to his right-hand side.

To his right-hand side…

Perched on the edge of the ridge, the boulder was about twenty feet across and ten feet high. Beelzebub Jones slow-crawled to his left, inched around the edge of the boulder and took up a firing position behind a pile of rocks.

A hundred feet away, two gunmen broke cover, firing rifles from the hip as they advanced towards him.

"See you in hell, boys." Beelzebub Jones sighted his Winchester and in the space between two heartbeats both men dropped to the ground.

Scrabbling further to his left, Beelzebub Jones rose to a kneeling position, took a bead on two more gunmen, exhaled slowly and blew their heads apart. Arcing to his right he laid down suppressing fire, his right hand a blur, cocking the lever with practiced ease. And then, in a single fluid motion, he stood, turned and sprinted towards a boulder, bullets raising dust around him as he dived for cover.

And then the firing stopped, the final gunshot echoing away across the desert.

"Beelzebub Jones," yelled a voice. "This is the sheriff of Trinity. You're pinned down, son. You may as well come out and give yourself up."

Behind the rock, Beelzebub Jones reloaded the Winchester. "Now sheriff," he shouted.

"You know that ain't gonna happen. I killed your posse and I'm coming for you next."

"I wouldn't be too sure about that, son. I got more guns'n you have."

The sheriff's voice had changed position. Beelzebub Jones readied himself.

"This is your last chance, Jones…"

Beelzebub Jones hung his Stetson on the barrel of the Winchester and lifted it slowly above the boulder. A gunshot rang out, and as the Stetson flew through the air, he stood, aimed and fired off two shots. The sheriff dropped where he stood, blood gouting from what remained of his head.

Grinning to himself, Beelzebub Jones stepped out from behind the boulder and looked around.

"The sheriff's dead," he yelled. "If there's anyone left you got five seconds to show yourself."

The desert rang with silence as vultures began to circle overhead, drawn by the blood scent of dead lawmen.

"Reach for your gun."

Beelzebub Jones whirled towards the sound of the voice, his Winchester clattering to the ground as Colt .45s appeared in each hand.

No one there.

Turning slowly, every sense alive, he surveyed the area, eyes searching for movement, ears straining for the slightest sound.

Silence.

"Come on out," he shouted.

"I have come to end you."

Beelzebub Jones whirled again. "Who's there," he said. "Show yourself."

"I will end you," said the voice. "You are the unholy one. I am the cure."

The dry, desert air chilled as a mist descended; swirling clarity into an otherworldly confusion of foreboding that resonated deep within Beelzebub Jones, enveloping him with menace, filling him with uncertainty.

And then the mist fell away, as a stiff breeze moaned across the ridge, lifting vortexes of dust and scudding tumbleweed along the ground.

As the breeze settled a figure appeared.

A tall cowboy; some fifty feet away, face shaded beneath the brim of a large white Stetson, dressed in a pristine white shirt with pearl buttons tucked into a white denim pants held by a studded leather belt over which hung a single-holster housing the largest revolver Beelzebub Jones had ever seen.

Beneath the harsh sunlight, the cowboy struck a messianic figure. But his pose was unmistakable, arms loose, fingers flexing. The stance of a gunfighter.

So be it.

Beelzebub Jones grinned as he holstered his .45s. "And who the hell are you?"

The figure lifted his chin. "They call me the Man-in-White," he said. "You're the disease and I'm the cure. I've come to end you."

"End me?" said Beelzebub Jones. "How's that gonna work?"

"We're gonna draw. You're gonna die."

"Them's bold words, mister. Look around at the lawmen lyin' dead by my hand. I am chaos unfurled, son."

"We're gonna draw," said the Man-in-White. "You're gonna die."

The time for talk was over. Silence fell, save for the lonesome "Screeee…" of a Golden Eagle high above them.

Beelzebub Jones stared hard into the middle distance, but his periphery locked onto the other's hands.

The Man-in-White made his move but Beelzebub Jones drew first, firing both Colt .45s. The Man-in-White staggered backwards, jolted by the impact of four bullets to the chest, then steadied himself and drew his handgun.

White flame erupted from the barrel with a sound like a dynamite explosion in a mineshaft.

Beelzebub Jones flew backwards, spinning around from the sledgehammer punch to his right shoulder. Lying in the dirt, ears ringing from the gunshot blast, he woke from a daze to a sinister chirring sound. Opening his eyes he forced himself to stay calm as the chirring became louder, more insistent. Three feet away from his head a rattlesnake lifted from its coils into strike position.

Behind him, heavy footsteps moved closer.

"I am the cure."

The rattlesnake's tail blurred at the sound of the voice, it's warning now deafening, its body arcing slowly as if in a deadly ballet.

"And now you die."

Beelzebub Jones visualised the Man-in-White extending his arm, heard the loud metallic click as he drew back the hammer, smiling as braced himself for the end.

"Say goodbye."

Wings folded, dropping from a thousand feet, the Golden Eagle hit the Man-in-White's arm with the force of a cannonball. The gunshot erupted a crater in the ground, and as the Man-in-White struggled to fend off repeated attacks from the huge raptor, the rattlesnake extended to its full length, burying its fangs into his leg.

"We will come."

Galvanised by the chaos, Beelzebub Jones staggered to his feet, clutched his ruined arm and for the first time in his existence, he turned and ran.

As he disappeared between a group of boulders, the Golden Eagle launched into the air, its huge wings flapping lazily, lifting it easily towards the sky. His arms now free, the Man-in-White grasped the rattlesnake behind its head and tore it from its grip, ripping flesh from his shin that cascaded blood over his boot.

Throwing the snake to one side, the Man-in-White limped towards the boulders.

Beelzebub Jones stumbled on beneath the harsh sun, blood pouring from the remnant of his shoulder. Ahead, the path narrowed. On one side a sheer rock face. On the other, a hundred-foot drop to the river below. Breathless and dizzy, his vision darkening around the edges, he leaned against the rock face, breath rasping as he fought to drag air into his lungs.

His vision clearing, Beelzebub Jones forced himself upright, swayed drunkenly, and then, as the dizziness subsided, set off again.

The bullet hit him with the force of a steam train, punching a hole between his shoulder blades, and as he flew through the air the last thing he remembered was the echo of the gunshot fading across the desert.

*****

The river stained red as the fierce current rolled and tumbled Beelzebub Jones' broken, lifeless body against jagged rocks that smashed bone and contorted snapped limbs into grotesque shapes.

Further downstream, thirteen vultures dropped from the sky; forming a wake at the water's edge, hungry to feast on the fresh carrion leaking blood into the shallows of Lake Placid. Emboldened by the scent of the cadaver the largest scavenger lifted into the air, flapped clumsily over the body and then returned to the wake. All thirteen vultures turned their heads as one as the ground began to tremble.

A quarter mile away, a form emerged from the heat shimmer, its fluid outline solidifying into a snorting, whinnying, pale mustang, thundering towards them at full gallop.

The vultures scattered as the mustang splashed into the shallows, whickering softly as it nudged the body towards the center of the lake.

Reaching deeper water, the mustang swam downstream, stooped to position itself beneath the floating corpse then stood upright, lifting Beelzebub Jones onto its back before returning to shallows and then walking out of the lake towards the heat shimmer.

Dead Man's Hand

The antechamber fell silent as Beelzebub Jones laid down his cards. Demonic gasps rippled around the table as, one by one, he turned up two black eights, two black aces and the queen of clubs. "Eights and aces," he said. "Read 'em and weep, boys."

Across the table, the hooded figure lifted its head slowly; eyes burning red, lips parting to reveal death-yellow fangs.

"You win again." The growl of its voice sounded like distant peals of thunder, and yet dripped with the charm that had cheated a thousand souls. "Another hand?" it said. "Double up or quit? Double stake or split?"

Beelzebub Jones shook his head. "By your grace, I got somewhere to be. I'ma quit while I'm ahead," he said. "That was the deal."

The hooded figure stroked its goatee and then tipped its head in acquiescence. "The deal stands," it waved a dismissive hand. "Win some, lose some, it's all the same to me."

Beelzebub Jones thanked each player in turn, and with a final nod, stood up and backed slowly out of the antechamber, his eyes never leaving the hooded figure. Once through the stone entrance he waited until the huge oak door slammed shut before turning around.

The Great Hall flickered in the light of a hundred burning souls impaled on stout pikes fashioned from cedar, pine and cypress. Each retaining its human form, each face contorted in the anguished screams of a soul in eternal fiery torment.

At the far end of the hall, arched by fire, a huge portcullis began to rise. Ironwork glowing red, lifted by clanking chains driven by a huge capstan powered by a dozen more condemned souls, their filthy bodies lashed to bloody pulp by a demon with a flaming bullwhip.

Beelzebub Jones started walking. Beyond the gate, a monstrous two-headed dog stood guard, staring out across an ink-black river. As Beelzebub Jones approached, the dog turned and growled as it moved reluctantly to one side.

A boat appeared. Twenty feet long, ten feet at its beam and piloted from the stern by a cloaked figure, his features shrouded by a dark hood. Beelzebub Jones stepped aboard and dropped two silver dollars into the pilot's outstretched hand. Secreting the coins within the folds of his cloak, the pilot nodded once and began to propel the boat silently across the river.

Return To The Crossing Place

Beelzebub Jones stepped out of the boat and onto a dilapidated jetty that led to a wooden bridge stretching across a dark abyss, its parallel lines converging at a ball of white fire glowing in the distance.

A seemingly endless stream of the recently-departed trudged towards him along the bridge, herded to eternal damnation by demonic riders astride growling hell beasts, lashing the condemned souls with bullwhips or prodding with lances, the tips of which glowed with white heat.

As they filed past, Beelzebub Jones nodded cheerfully, tipping his Stetson at preachers, bankers, lawyers and politicians, winking at outlaws and murderers. "It ain't as bad as you think, boys," he said. "The first ten thousand years are the worst. After that it's a breeze."

As he walked along the bridge, his boots marked his pace on the ancient oak boards.

Clomp.

Clomp.

Clomp.

With each step he took, the white fireball grew larger.

Clomp.

Clomp.

Clomp.

A multitude of flames dancing and flickering within a transparent sphere.

Clomp.

Clomp.

Clomp.

The size of a stagecoach.

Clomp.

Clomp.

Clomp

The size of a house.

Close up, the fireball filled his vision. A wall of flames stretching up to the sky. As he drew closer still the flames parted to open an archway in front of him. Beelzebub Jones stepped through and continued walking along the bridge.

Clomp.

Clomp-thump.

Clomp-thump.

Thump.

Thump.

Thump.

Thump-ump.

Thump-ump.

Thump-ump.

Beelzebub Jones opened his eyes to the sound of the drumbeat, and the familiar earthen smell of dried tobacco leaves that covered his bare midriff.

He was inside a large Tipi. Arcane symbols and naïve artwork daubed on buffalo hides that rippled in the slight desert breeze. Smoked drifted lazily upwards, drawn towards the hole at the apex of the poles.

He tried to move but found himself bound securely to a simple bed fashioned from branches and animal skins.

Beelzebub Jones cursed as he tried to move against his binds.

"Well you took your damn time."

Beelzebub Jones' eyes searched for The Stranger. "I couldn't get away," he said. "Got into a poker game with the devil. Aces and eights, and I got to walk out." He looked around. "How did I get back here?"

"Same as last time," said The Stranger. "Your horse brung you. Dragged you out of the lake and walked three days through the desert."

"When can I get outta here?"

"When I say so."

Beelzebub Jones tried to move again. "How come I'm tied up?"

"You gotta heal, son," said The Stranger. "You got your ass kicked this time. Broke perty much every bone you got when you fell off that cliff. You was as good as dead before you hit the water."

"How's that possible? Last time we met you told me I was the infernal chosen one?"

"Turns out there is another," said The Stranger.

Beelzebub Jones tried to clear the cobwebs from his memory. "You mean that bastard who shot me? I put four in his chest before he could move, and then he drew his gun. One shot and I thought he'd blown my fucking arm off."

"That's The-Man-in-White," said The Stranger.

"Hadn't been for a rattlesnake and an eagle he'd a done for me."

"Shapeshifters," said The Stranger.

"Do what now?"

"The Cherokee and the African gal," said The Stranger. "They took on the form of the eagle and the rattlesnake. Bought you some time by all accounts."

Beelzebub Jones grunted. "Hornswoggled and shot in the back," he said. "Must be losing my touch." He paused. "So who'd you say that bastard was?"

"The Man in White. He's your nemesis."

"My what?"

"Your equal," The Stranger said. "And… your opposite. He's the only one who can kill you."

"If he's my equal," said Beelzebub Jones. "does that mean I'm the only one who can kill him?"

"Maybe," said The Stranger.

"Only maybe? The fucker shot me in the back, I ain't lettin' that go."

"If you want to kill him, you're gonna need a gun like his," said The Stranger. "It's a god-killer."

"A god-killer?"

"It's called The Revelator. Never needs reloading, and spits out black flame."

"Where can I get one?"

"All in good time," said The Stranger. "You gotta heal first."

******

Forty days later, Beelzebub Jones woke to sunlight blowing dust motes through a gap in the Tipi's hide. He looked around, and then down at himself. His binds were gone, his shoulder a mass of shiny scar tissue. After tentatively flexing his fingers and limbs he sat up, swung his body around until his feet were on the floor.

"How you feelin'?"

"About ready to kill somethin'," said Beelzebub Jones. "And I wanna start with the bastard who shot me in the back. But I need one of them guns."

"The Revelator," said The Stranger."

"Where do I get one?"

"There is only one other."

Beelzebub Jones sighed. "I ain't never been blessed with any kind of patience," he said. "But what scrap I do have is bein' stretched mighty thin. Now, I'ma ask you one more time. Where do I get me a Revelator?"

"The church of St. Barnabus," said The Stranger. "Beneath the floor where the preacher stands there's a chamber of stone. You gotta blow that open to find a chest made of iron. Then you gotta blow the lid off the chest to get to the Revelator."

"The church of St. Barnabus?" said Beelzebub Jones. "Where I kilt that preacher?"

"That's right," said The Stranger. "I figured no one would look in a church for a god-killin' gun, and if they did find it, it wouldn't be easy to open."

Beelzebub Jones frowned. "You hid the gun in the church? So you had it all the time?"

"Yep."

"Then why in the name of Sam Hill didn't you keep a hold of it and give it straight to me?"

"I figured blowing up a church might improve your mood."

Gabby

Beelzebub Jones saddled up, mounted his mustang and headed towards Trinity. About a mile from town he came across a broken-down wooden shack right where The Stranger said it would be. Outside the shack, a tied-up mule stood forlornly amidst a carnage of broken furniture, rusty tools, split barrels and the remains of a cart.

Taking a good look around, Beelzebub Jones dismounted, picked his way through the detritus and stepped up onto the porch. The screen door, its panels torn and useless, hung drunkenly in the doorway. Loud, rattling snores, together with the unholy stench of a man past his prime, emanated from within the shack.

Dust and termites fell from the doorframe, disturbed by the hammering of Beelzebub Jones's fist. "Gabby, GABBY. You in there?"

The snores continued.

Beelzebub Jones thought for a moment. "Wake up ol' timer,' he yelled. "I got whiskey."

The snoring stopped, replaced by grunts of wet-brain confusion. "Who'sh that? Who'sh out there?"

"I need your help, Gabby. Why don't you come on out?"

More shuffling and then a tiny, grey whiskered old man appeared squinting in the doorway. "Whishkey, you shay?" His words whistled between blackened teeth like a foul wind in a graveyard. He peered closer. "I know you," he said.

Beelzebub Jones took a step back. Tried not to breathe. "Like I said, I need your help," he said.

The old man's eyes flashed with low animal cunning. "Wha'sh in it for me?"

"A bottle of whiskey," said Beelzebub Jones. "And a couple of silver dollars for that sportin' gal you like in the Wormy Dog."

"And what's that gonna getcha?"

"A pick axe, your mule," Beelzebub Jones paused. "And a shitload of dynamite."

Gabby blinked. "Dynamite, you say?"

"'s 'at a problem?"

"No sir," Gabby said. "No problem."

"You know where t'get some?"

Gabby winked and tapped his nose. "Got 'er right here," he said.

Beelzebub Jones looked around. "You got dynamite here?"

"Sure, why not?"

"Where do you keep it?"

Gabby gurned a smile. "Got a crate 'neath my bed, had her a while now."

A thousand questions lined up in Beelzebub Jones' head, but he chose just one. "Will it still blow shit up?"

An hour later, Beelzebub Jones headed the mustang towards Trinity. Behind them, Gabby's mule, toting a wooden crate stencilled with skull and crossbones, plodded reluctantly at the end of the longest rope they could find.

Blowing Up The Church

The Church of St. Barnabus was a tired-looking wooden building about a mile or so from Trinity. Faded white paint flaked like a skin disease from its rotting structure.

Beelzebub Jones dismounted, secured the mustang to a fence post, and then walked over to the mule and untied the wooden crate and pickaxe from the saddle. Lowering the crate gingerly to the ground, he pried the lid off to reveal rows of red dynamite sticks packed in straw. Lifting two sticks from the crate, he turned, strode towards the church and pushed open the door.

"Come on in," said a voice.

A young priest stood by the altar. He smiled as Beelzebub Jones walked towards him along the narrow aisle.

"All are welcome in the house of God," said the priest.

Beelzebub Jones grunted. "Hold on to that thought," he said. "I'm about to place some dynamite right where you're standin'."

"I – what?"

"Step aside, preacher. I ain't got much time, and I ain't sure how stable these here sticks might be."

The priest stared open-mouthed. "You bring dynamite into a sacred place?" he said. "I will not allow this…"

The Colt .45 appeared in Beelzebub Jones' right hand. "Preacher," he said. "Last time I was in here, bein' a priest didn't count for a hill of beans. You can either help me out, walk out now, or prepare to meet thy maker."

He paused. "An' that's two more options than the last preacher got."

The young priest gulped and stood to one side.

Beelzebub Jones nodded as he holstered the revolver, "good choice." He stepped towards an oak table covered with a white cloth embroidered with crosses in red silk.

"This the altar?"

The priest looked confused. "What?"

213

"This table with the fancy cloth," said Beelzebub Jones. "Is this the altar?"

"Ye-yes," stammered the priest. "It was shipped over from Rome, sent by the Holy Father himself, it…"

Beelzebub Jones walked around the altar, inspected it closely, nodded and then crawled beneath it. Seconds later he straightened up. "Thanks for your help, preacher," he said. "Guess I'll be getting along."

Halfway to the door, he turned. "You might want to follow me," he said. "No telling when that dynamite's gonna blow."

The priest saw the smoke fizzing from beneath the altar, looked up at Beelzebub Jones, back at the altar and then, with a yelp of horror sprinted towards the church door.

The explosions blew out the church windows in a blast of glass fragments, wood splinters and dust. When the cloud settled, Beelzebub Jones picked up two more dynamite sticks and walked back into the church, stepping over broken chairs towards the crater where the altar had stood.

"What have you done?" The priest stared ashen-faced at the damage.

"Blew me a hole in the floor," said Beelzebub Jones. "That was a damn sturdy altar, preacher man. Directed the blast downwards." He looked around the church. "Mostly."

He peered into the crater. "Yep, there she is."

Three feet down, a metal box, about the size of a child's coffin, lay amidst lumps of stone and splintered floorboards.

"Hot damn, right where he said it would be." Beelzebub Jones clog-danced a few steps of triumph and then hopped into the crater. A brief inspection showed that the metal box was undamaged but too heavy to lift. The lid held tightly shut by a haft and staple of forged steel and secured with a brass padlock the size of a man's fist.

"Ain't nothin' else for it." Beelzebub Jones positioned the dynamite behind the padlock, lit the fuses and scrambled out of the crater.

215

This time, the explosion took out the end wall and half of the roof. A couple of seconds later the priest yelped again as the twisted and smoking remains of the padlock hit the ground a short distance from where he stood.

Beelzebub Jones regarded the mangled lock with a raised eyebrow. "Guess she'll open now," he said.

Apart from a blackened dent where the lock had been, the strongbox looked to be intact. The heavy lid screeched reluctantly open to reveal a hessian sack filled with sand. Beelzebub Jones removed the sandbag and whistled in admiration.

Inside the strongbox lay an ornate leather shoulder holster; its seams riveted with gleaming brass studs; the front panel embossed with the image of Stetson-bedecked outlaw skull, its lower features masked by a kerchief, the design set against crossed revolvers. As a piece of artwork it was remarkable, but Beelzebub Jones had eyes only for the huge pistol grip that protruded from the holster.

"What kinda gun is that?"

Beelzebub Jones looked up at the priest's voice. "This's more than just a gun," he said.

He lifted the holster from the strong box and slipped it over his shoulder, arranging and adjusting the leather straps until the holster fit snugly beneath his left armpit. Once the outfit was comfortable, Beelzebub Jones' hand reached across, drew the weapon and stared at it in awe.

The huge revolver shone like the sun. Its barrel slightly longer than a Colt .45, but with the bore of a Winchester rifle. The fat cylinder span with a smooth, well-engineered, metallic whir; each one of its eight chambers an unblinking eye that stared with menace, black as the entrance to hell.

Beelzebub Jones' face split into a childlike grin. "Behold the Revelator," he said.

"What are you gonna do with it?" said the priest.

Beelzebub Jones' grin faded to an expression that the priest never wanted to see again. "I'm gonna get me some retribution," he said.

He turned to the priest. "You speak Spanish, preacher man?"

"Si," smiled the priest.

"And are you familiar in the ways of writin'?"

The priest frowned. "Of course," he said. "At the seminary I was praised for the penmanship of my sermons, and furthermore…"

His words faded beneath the glare of Beelzebub Jones' expression. The priest cleared his throat. "Why do you ask?"

"Cos I got some instructions for you. You listen to what I'm gonna tell you, and then you get on and do it. To the letter."

Trinity

Two nights later, the townsfolk of Trinity lined both sides of Main Street, waiting in silent expectation, their faces glowing in the flickering light of burning torches positioned every few feet all the way to the Wormy Dog saloon.

Beelzebub Jones felt their eyes upon him, heard the occasional mutter as the mustang carried him slowly past. As he rode by he smiled to himself, the preacher had done his job.

"Hold it right there, Jones."

The sheriff stepped from a crowd on the boardwalk outside the Wormy Dog, walked to the middle of the street, turned and cocked his Winchester.

Beelzebub Jones halted the mustang. "Evenin' sheriff. Don't believe we've been acquainted yet?" He looked around the town. "Looks like quite the welcoming committee."

The sheriff smirked. "The only welcome you're gonna find is down in hell, just after we send you back." He glanced back at the saloon. "Ain't that right boys?"

A dozen deputies, all carrying Winchesters, walked out onto Main Street and lined up next to the sheriff.

Hearing a noise behind him, Beelzebub Jones turned in his saddle. Twenty yards away, a dozen more deputies walked out onto the street, each carrying a Winchester.

He turned back to the sheriff. "This town sure has a lot of rifles. You mind if step down from my horse? I'd like him outta the way before it starts gettin' unpleasant."

The sheriff nodded. "You can step down, but do it slow."

With exaggerated care, Beelzebub Jones dismounted, looped the reins around the pommel and leaned close to the mustang's ear. "You're the best damn horse, I ever had," he whispered. "But I guess you knew that."

He turned to the deputies standing behind him. "I'm gonna send my horse on his way," he said. "The first one tries to stop him will be the first one to die. We clear on that?"

"Let the horse go."

Beelzebub Jones nodded to the sheriff, stroked the mustang's mane and then slapped its hindquarter. "Go on, get,"

The mustang whinnied, then turned and galloped through the line of deputies and headed out of town.

When the sound of hoofbeats faded to silence, Beelzebub Jones strolled to the center of

Main Street and turned to the sheriff. "So, how's this gonna play?"

The lawman shrugged. "You're gonna end up dead. Easiest way is to give yourself up."

Beelzebub Jones nodded. "Figured you might say that. But I'ma tell you this, every man that lifts a gun against me tonight is gonna die."

"Them's bold words," said the sheriff. "'cept it looks like we're holdin' all the cards. This is your last chance. Drop your guns and…"

His words tailed off, his face twisting in horror twisting at the freakish, nightmare vision of the outlaw transforming into a skeletal monster.

Cackling with hysterical glee, Beelzebub Jones drew both Colt .45s, spinning them around bony forefingers in a blur of chrome as he turned slowly, arms outstretched, revelling in the shock on the faces of the lawmen.

And then the guns stopped spinning.

The sheriff was the first to die. his horrified expression disappearing in an explosion of blood, the Colts spitting fire in a rapid fusillade so fierce that when hammers clicked against empty chambers, eleven more deputies bled their last into the dust.

As his empty revolvers clattered to the ground, Beelzebub Jones reached for the shoulder holster, and then everything went black.

Revelations

Face down on Main Street, Beelzebub Jones woke to the sound of voices.

"He, he ain't dead."

"But I shot him in the head."

"It was a misfire, you dumb shit. I saw the bullet bounce off his skull."

As he listened he felt faint vibrations in the ground. Confused at first, he flattened his hands against the dirt. The vibrations came again, stronger this time, and he smiled to himself as realisation dawned.

Wiping dust from his mouth he rolled over to see a circle of the surviving lawmen, all of them pointing Winchesters at his head.

"You got any last words before we send you back to hell, you sonofabitch?"

Desiccated sinews pulled Beelzebub Jones' skeletal features into the semblance of a grin. "Listen to that, boys," he said.

The vibrations grew in magnitude, the ground shuddering in time with the relentless thunder of approaching hoof beats overlaid with the banshee screams of indigent war cries, ululations from the birthplace of mankind; and a fearsome volley of rifle fire that dropped six lawmen where they stood.

Beelzebub Jones rolled clear just before the Apocalypse Riders ploughed into the remaining deputies, flailing hooves snapping spines and shattering bones as they trampled them into the dirt.

Stooping to collect his revolvers, he speed-loaded and holstered both Colts and walked out into the center of Main Street.

"I came here for one thing," he yelled. "I sent a message to the sheriff that I wanted a gunfight with the Man-in-White, one on one." He paused, took a breath as he stared at the cowed townsfolk. "But the sheriff set up this ambush and now all these lawmen are dead. That's on him."

He paused again, flexing his fingers as he seemed to consider what to say next.

"I know you can hear me," he yelled. "So come out now and face me. If you don't, there's gonna be some more killing done." Beelzebub Jones nodded towards the Apocalypse Riders. "My friends here are gonna see to that."

He fell silent. Fear hung like a cloak over the expectant townsfolk, Beelzebub Jones smiled as he followed their eyes.

Lifting his head he called again, his voice louder. "I know you're in the Wormy Dog. This is your last chance, you yellow sonofabitch, come on out and fight me."

For several long seconds nothing happened, and then the bat-wing saloon doors creaked and the Man-in-White stepped out onto the wooden boardwalk.

"I'm here," he said. His voice clear, confident. "Leave them folks alone, they ain't done nothin' to you."

He strolled towards the center of Main Street.

For a few seconds each sized up the other, and then Beelzebub Jones nodded towards the Revelator hung low down on the Man-in-White's hip. "Kind of a heavy piece to wear like that, doncha think?" he said. "Especially in a gunfight."

The Man-in-White swallowed his doubt and deadpanned his response. "Don't you worry about me," he said. "Only one of us is gonna walk away from this. Right will prevail and you'll end up exactly where you belong."

"You keep telling yourself that. I bested you last time, an' I'm gonna best you this time."

The Man-in-White smiled. "It's over. The cards were against you from the day you were born. You spent your life in a cesspit of nicotine, liquor, blasphemy; shrouded in a cloak of death and depravity."

He took a breath, his confidence building. "You are nothing," he said. "I am the light."

Beelzebub Jones stared ahead, his body as still as a corpse.

The smile twisted into a sneer. "Your very name belongs to the devil, he said. "Given to you by

225

a fornicating sow who spent her life on her back or inside a bottle of gin."

He paused. "You got nothing to say about that?"

Beelzebub Jones lifted his head. "I got something to say."

Townsfolk gasped at the menace in his voice, and then Trinity fell silent.

Beelzebub Jones flexed his fingers. "Reach for your gun, motherfucker."

It was over in a finger-snap; but he saw the detail of every moment in breath-taking clarity. He saw the hand reach down to the white leather holster, saw the fingers curl around the grip, saw the wrist muscle tense, saw the Revelator raise towards him, saw the gunsight of his own Revelator, felt the pressure of the trigger, heard the thunderous boom, saw the jet of black flame, inhaled the sulphurous odor of gunsmoke, and saw the hole appear in the Man-in-White's chest.

As his body lurched backwards, the Man-in-White's Revelator flew upwards, moonlight flashing against the metal as it twisted and spun through the air. Beelzebub Jones sighted again, squeezed the trigger, and then closed his eyes and stretched his arms wide to stand before what was to come.

His bullet hit the Revelator square on its chamber, detonating an explosion like the sound of planets colliding that obliterated the town of Trinity in a burning maelstrom of dust, broken glass, splintered wood and human flesh.

Cruciform, his face lifted to the sky, Beelzebub Jones shrieked with delight at the punch of the sound wave, and began to scream exaltation to the Son of Perdition as the rolling thunder of the firestorm passed around and over him.

Other voices joined him. Opening his eyes, he found himself astride his mustang, to his left the Maasai Princess gazed at the sky, ululating in rapture to the ancestors of creation. To his right, Apache and Cherokee warriors sang songs of devotion to the Great Spirit as the world began to burn.

And then the horses reared, turned as one and with hellish cries the Apocalypse Riders spurred their mounts and as they galloped towards the night sky five playing cards fluttered to the ground; two black eights, two black aces and the queen of clubs.

*****

In the Chapel of Bones the little girl looked up to the priest. Her voice barely a whisper. "¿Qué está pasando padre?" she said.

The priest made the sign of the cross for the last time and then removed his collar.

"Revelaciones, hija mía," he said. "Revelaciones."

Expense Account

When the MP's expenses scandal first hit the newspapers it was reported that one charming Right Honourable Member had claimed for the poppy he wore on Remembrance Day. At the time the British Army were suffering losses in Afghanistan due to lack of proper kit. This poem was printed in the Daily Mail, I still have mixed feelings about that.

"We're proud of our troops,"
They say to the camera,
As you crouch in a firefight,
In a hot desert land.

"We all must stand firm,"
They say to the camera,
Yet they rarely set foot,
Into Afghanistan.

"They're the best in the world,"
They say to the camera,
As they take all your money,
To bail out the banks.

"It's another sad loss,"
They say to the camera,
As they send you to battle,
In obsolete tanks.

"*We will remember,*"
They say to the camera,
As they lay down a wreath,
In your dead comrade's name.

"*We will remember,*"
They say to the camera,
With a receipt for the poppy,
To attach to a claim.

How can they stand there,
And speak to the camera,
And say what they say,
And keep a straight face?

They're not worthy to speak,
In your name to the camera,
When their actions at home,
Are a fucking disgrace.

Funny Car

Cars feature a lot in my stories; especially fast, American cars. This story reflects my love for the noise and spectacle of drag-racing, and is part-inspired by an event that I witnessed at Long Marston Raceway back in the 1980s.
This goes out to Tom Coe.

No one would call it elegant, not by any means.

Brutal and uncompromising, certainly. Beautiful in its own way perhaps. But not elegant.

It was your classic example of form following function. Its form was a streamlined carbon-fibre shell attached to a chassis. Its function was to transport me from a standing start to over 300 mph in five seconds, over a distance of a quarter of a mile and hopefully get me there before the other car.

She was called 'Black Dog' and she was my Top Fuel Funny Car.

For those with no idea what I'm talking about, a Funny Car is a type of dragster that loosely resembles a normal car but with huge wheels at the back, skinny wheels at the front and a massive engine in between.

'Black Dog' resembled a 1970 Dodge Charger, a classic American car with looks and performance that would make your hair curl. Her fans loved her and every race would result in a flurry of messages left on our website.

To the enthusiast, there's something about a muscle car that stirs the emotions, makes the heart beat just that little bit faster, and 'Black Dog' was a carbon fibre supermodel, long, low and black with a big red 62 painted on each side.

As always, though, it's what lies beneath that counts; lift the body shell and you'd see a tubular chassis with a front-mounted Chrysler 426 Hemi engine, bored out to 500 cubic inches - that's about eight litres in real money.

On top of the engine, a Roots supercharger sits on the carburetors and inhales through a huge stainless-steel air scoop with a mouth that gapes like a fledgling demanding to be fed.

Add in a mixture of nitromethane and methanol (that's the Top Fuel bit) and you've got 8000 horsepower good to go.

Yeah, I'm a petrol-head, you may have noticed; have been for as long as I can remember. As a small child I used to go to the library and borrow books about engines. At ten years old I could explain how a turbocharger worked. At twelve years old my dad bought an old Morris Minor and showed me how to strip it down and rebuild it.

I grew up in England in the seventies. Back then you could get magazines like 'Custom Car', 'Street Machine' and 'Hot Rod and Custom'. I saw an advert for a trainee mechanic at a small garage that built and modified engines for dragsters. I got the job and soon after, built my first car and began racing.

After a while I began to win more than I lost and managed to get enough sponsorship to build and run a Funny Car. 'Black Dog' was my first proper dragster, and now my last.

Every race feels like the first time; fear, excitement, exhilaration rush like you wouldn't believe. There's nothing like it.

You begin with a burnout, which is basically a wheel-spin to heat the tyres and lay down some rubber on the track for increased traction. Lots of noise, lots of smoke - the crowds love it.

Then you back the car up and inch forward to the starting line, keeping your eyes on the Christmas Tree, that's what we call the starting lights.

The blue light at the top means that you're in the correct position to start the race. Below that are three amber lights and a green light. These light in sequence, half a second apart from top to bottom.

Let me tell you, there's no better feeling in the world than starting a drag race.

Your fireproof hood and crash helmet muffle all sounds except your quickening pulse and the dull rumble of the engine. The safety harness straps you tight into the seat, transmitting every movement through your body. All you can see is the sun glinting on the air scoop, a quarter of a mile beyond that is the finishing line.

But your focus is on the Christmas Tree.

Blue.

Amber.

Amber.

Amber.

GREEN.

Foot to the floor and BOOM! your world explodes. Flames spit from the exhaust pipes and the big supercharged V8 bellows as it accelerates you to 6G. The finishing post races towards you, the only tangible reference in your world of noise, vibration and a blurred backdrop of Warp Factor Three, Mr. Sulu.

Full throttle for five seconds and two parachutes to slow you down.

You hope.

I've lost count of the number of times I've raced. Hundreds of starts at dozens of strips both here and abroad, never had one incident.

Until last week.

Everything seemed to be fine. Black Dog leapt forward on green and then I remember a flash from the engine, followed by smoke and flames, a brief glimpse of the sky and then nothing.

Sometime afterwards, I heard a voice say that the engine backfired and then exploded, sending a piece of shrapnel through one of the rear tyres and sending the car out of control.

Another voice said that I hit a concrete barrier at 300mph and that I'm lucky to be alive.

Black Dog was destroyed of course. Nothing left worth repairing. I felt sad when I heard that; I believe cars have souls, you see. Maybe I'll find out.

My wife and kids visit every day. Sitting by my bed, holding my hand and telling me everything that's going on at home and at school. My youngest daughter is a three-year-old angel; she loves to climb on my bed, put her face close to mine and tell me what we're all going to do when I leave hospital.

Tonight, just before they all left, she hugged me tight and whispered that she loves me and she just wants me to wake up. As I look down at them gathered around me, my heart is filled with love for my beautiful family.

This is the last time I shall see them or hear their voices.

I just wish I could say goodbye.

Eighty-Four

Number 84 is a teashop in Gravesend, frequented by Emma Dehaney (editor of Burdizzo Books) and home to the No. 84 Writing Group. In 2019 they invited me to submit to a collection of stories of 84 words.

He stared at her across the table; as beautiful now as she was in 1940.

Arthritic fingers shook as he read the perfume-scented letter. Eyes welled at the words she had written on her 84th birthday in 2004.

The sentiments of a young girl, trapped in the cancer scrawl of a breathing cadaver.

He took the tablets from his pocket, stirred each one into the teacup, looked across at the empty chair, smiled for the last time and lifted the teacup to his lips.

Hank Williams' Cadillac

Country singer Hank Williams died in the back seat of his Cadillac in 1953, aged 29. The story of the manner of his passing got me thinking about other famous car-related deaths, and what happened to the cars.

It was my buddy Stu who came up with the idea.

My name's Vince, and this story began when we embarked on a road trip.

We were 19-year-old high-school drop-outs and occasionally reformed stoners sharing a broke-down, drunk-leaning, leaky old double-wide on a third-world trailer-park in a small town in Nowhere, Texas.

Sometimes in life you don't know where you're headed until you get there, that's when you have to decide if it's where you want to be. Turns out we ended up in entry-level jobs at Walmart. That was two years ago. Need I say more?

Notwithstanding our ongoing education from life and the internet - majoring in popular culture and low animal cunning - two years of the real world made us realise that maybe we should've made more of an effort at school.

As a fat man once said, "It is what it is."

It was late one Sunday evening, and Stu was getting mellow to quell the dread of another year-long week in retail, when he experienced a bong-inspired epiphany that he and I would join the US Marines. All we had to do was serve long enough to qualify for a college education, and then all our dreams would come true.

"Well, hell," I said. "That's random."

We had nothing to leave behind, Stu's mom was dead, and mine was in jail, partly for dealing in meth-amphetamines and Oxycontin, but mostly for trying to kill me (but that's a story for another day), and so we were raring to go, both of us excited to embark on this next stage of our lives.

Anyway, as a kind of last hurrah to civilian life we decided to set out to explore the back roads of the Texas boondocks and see if we could get some anecdotes under our belts before the maelstrom that we knew would befall us at Boot

Camp. We'd heard horror stories from "One-eyed Joe", an enigmatic Marine Corps veteran with a drink problem and a kickass record collection, who lived three trailers down from us.

Joe told us he was part Navajo, and wore a tattoo that said 'Semper Fi', and a USMC baseball cap that crowned a waist-length silver-grey pony tail. He also wore a dime-sized puckered scar just below his right shoulder, and a patch over his left eye, both of which he told us he got in 1968 at a place called Khe San.

Joe said he'd always been lucky.

Once our enlistment day was finalized, we organized the road trip and set out in Stu's 30-year-old, shit-box Honda Civic - he'd christened it "Brian", after Brian Wilson, claiming that Little Honda was his favourite Beach Boys song.

What can I say? When it comes to music, Stu is a borderline savant.

Anyhoo.

Day one passed without incident, culminating in a night spent first in a strip bar (thanks to a couple of forged IDs), and then in a dive bar next to a sleazy motel at a down-at-heel truck-stop, where Stu got lucky with a rinsed-out waitress called Irene.

We set off on day two, nursing weapons-grade hangovers. Around midday we'd passed the Cadillac Ranch on the I-40 just outside Amarillo. Stu slowed the car so we could pay homage to ten Cadillacs half-buried nose-deep in a field, and then informed me that the cars were positioned at an angle corresponding to that of the Great Pyramid of Giza in Egypt.

"No shit?" I said.

Once past the art installation, Stu found a country music station playing Johnny Cash back to back, whereupon he cranked up the music and buried his right foot. I fell asleep soon after.

When I woke up, we were driving in thick fog, immersed in a swirling cloud that coated the Honda in moisture that the windshield wipers struggled to clear. Soon after, the radio packed up, and then, crawling at ten miles per hour, the Honda suddenly lurched as the engine began making a clank-thump noise that sounded to me like a mechanical death rattle.

The car stumbled onwards, black exhaust-smoke staining the fog behind us.

"Shit," said Stu. "The temperature gauge is off the scale."

"How long's it been like that?" I said.

"Beats me, dude."

Great.

"We may as well keep it going," said Stu. "If we stop, we may not get it started again."

I had no argument with that and so we limped along for a while, wincing at the sound of mechanical carnage taking place deep inside the Honda's engine.

Eventually the fog began to disperse; thinning at first to reveal brief glimpses of a deserted Texas landscape, and then clearing completely as we approached a green road sign with serious gunshot wounds, and with defaced and weather-beaten writing that put me in mind of the last words of a dying man:

"Welcome to Rambling." It read.

"Where the holy fuck is Rambling?" said Stu.

My iPhone said 'No Service', so I opened the glove compartment.

"What are you looking for?" said Stu.

"A road atlas?" I said.

"Dude, seriously?"

Just as we passed the road sign the Honda backfired, lurched once and then rolled silently to halt at the side of the road, steam erupting from beneath the hood like the passing of its soul.

D.R.T. Dead Right There.

Stu grunted. "Well, that's the end of this suit."

We got out of the car. Behind us, the road converged to a shimmering vanishing point. Ahead of us sprawled a handful of tired-looking buildings, the closest of which was a used car lot, about a fifty yards away and bedecked with sun-faded and wind-tattered red, white and blue bunting that hung limply in the still morning air.

"I've still got no service," I said. "Let's go see if we can use their phone to call Triple-A."

"Triple-what?" said Stu.

Stuffing the Honda's keys in the back pocket of his jeans, he gave me a shit-eating grin as he donned fake Oakley wraparounds (a dollar-ninety-nine from Walmart), and then patted me on the shoulder. "It's all good, bro'," he said. "Maybe they got a mechanic who can fix us up?"

"Good luck with that," I said.

We set off towards the used car lot, Stu leading the way. As we drew closer, he whistled.

"Holy shit," he said. "Those are some sweet, sweet rides."

He was right. Every single automobile in the lot was an American classic. Ford Model B Coupes, Chevrolets with gleaming fenders, Cadillacs with sweeping fins. It was a cornucopia of chrome and whitewall tires. All the cars were in mint condition and not one was made after 1967.

At the front of the pack was a powder blue 1952 Cadillac convertible with Alabama plates. The roof was down and as we approached, a large crow settled on the top of the windshield, flapped its wings a couple times, folded them and then tilted

247

its head to one side, its beady eyes tracking us as we wandered around.

Stu checked out the license plate. "No way," he said.

"What?"

"This looks like Hank Williams' car."

"Hank Williams?" I said. "The country singer, Hank Williams? Your Cheatin' Heart and all that."

"Yeah."

"Are you serious?"

Stu took a breath. "I seen a picture of him sitting in a car just like this, and I recognise the license plate."

"Bullshit."

"Dude," he said. "How many powder blue Cadillac convertibles do you think were registered in Alabama in 1952?"

The crow lifted its wings and then settled, its head to one side, staring intently at Stu.

"That means nothing," I said.

Stu shook his head, grinning like a maniac.

"This is it, man. I'm telling you. This is Hank Williams' Cadillac."

"He ain't wrong," rasped the crow.

Stu and I did a comedy double-take and said, "What the fuck?" simultaneously.

"He ain't wrong."

The bird spoke with a sandpaper voice that put me in mind of Tom Waits after a night smoking Lucky Strikes.

Stu looked at me. "You heard that, right? Tell me you heard that."

"A talking bird," I said. "Well, shit just got weird."

The crow dipped its head a couple times, and then flapped its wings as it skittered for a few steps, lifted into the air, turned a 180, dropped back onto the windshield and then nodded towards the rear seat.

"Hank Williams croaked right there," it said.

Both Stu and I peered into the back of the Caddie. In the foot well lay a few beer cans and handwritten notes on scraps of paper.

"Mah associate is right."

Startled, I turned to see a tall, thin white man who looked about 60. He had thin, wispy hair, a white goatee, and wore a cream colored suit that had seen better days. He was sweating profusely and wiped his face several times with a large white handkerchief.

"Somewhere near Oak Hill, West Virginia, Hank Williams took his last breath, right on that back seat."

"D.R.T." said the crow. "Dead Right There."

The old guy's shabby appearance, and measured, polite southern accent put me in mind of a plantation owner who was down on his luck. Yet the glittering hardness and intensity of gaze from his steely blue eyes as they locked onto mine, raised hairs on the back of my head.

He extended his hand. "They call me Bubba," he said. "And this here's my car lot."

My mind was still trying to process the talking bird, but I heard myself ask, "where exactly are we, sir?"

Bubba winked. "You seen the road sign, son. This here's Rambling."

"Well, we're kinda lost," I said. "And our car's broke down. Can you maybe show us where are on a map?"

Bubba laughed once, and then gave a wink that made me shiver. "Oh, we ain't on no map, son."

"Well then, is there any place nearby that can take a look at our car?"

"All in good time, son," he said. "All in good time."

He turned to Stu. "I can see you are a man of discernment."

"That is one sick car, my man," said Stu.

"Interestin' choice of words."

Bubba gave another wink that walked over my grave.

"How much?" said Stu.

"Stu…" I began.

Bubba flashed me a look and then stepped between us.

"How much for what, son?" he said.

"This car," said Stu. "How much?"

"That depends, son. How bad do you want it?"

Stu shook his head. "It's a mighty fine automobile, an' I'm fairly certain I cain't afford it, but I'm kinda interested to know by how much."

I tried to step around to get to him, but Bubba placed a fatherly hand across Stu's shoulder and manoeuvred them both to a position that put their backs to me.

"Well," said Bubba. "In my experience, if you want something bad enough, then you'll find a way to afford it."

"You'll find a way," rasped the crow.

"Stu, we need to get going." I raised my voice, partly to get his attention, but mostly to hide the tremor of apprehension that hummed through my body.

I failed on both counts.

Bubba turned and gave me a terrible smile. "Son, your friend and I are in a business discussion, and besides, you ain't got a car. Where you gonna go? Now, we got a lotta fine automobiles in this lot, why don't you take a walk around and check 'em out?"

He turned his back on me and resumed inaudible muttering.

"Take a walk," rasped the crow.

Using up the last of my false bravado, I flipped the bird to the bird and then turned away. I reasoned that there was no way Stu was going to be able to afford to buy the Cadillac, so I may as well take a look around until he came to his senses.

I caught sight of an old car that looked to be from the 1920s. Up close it turned out to be an old Packard. Its square, wooden body looked like it belonged in a black and white gangster movie. Behind the Packard was a midnight blue Lincoln convertible with DC plates. Like the Caddie, the top was down, and at 20 feet long it was a whale of a car, with three rows of seats.

As I wandered around the lot, distracted by thoughts of talking birds, something about the random collection of cars sparked a glimpse of recognition, something I couldn't put my finger on.

Whatever.

I looked around. Bubba and Stu were nowhere to be seen, and I was about to head towards an old Porsche that I had spotted, when I heard voices.

At the rear of the lot was a small, single-storey office-building that I hadn't noticed before. I walked across to it, and glanced through the open door. Bubba was standing over Stu, who was sitting at a cheap wooden desk, holding a fountain pen that leaked what looked like red ink onto a piece of paper in front of him.

"Don't worry about that, son," chuckled Bubba. "All we need is your signature."

Bubba looked up, caught me staring and gave a grin that froze my heart. For the briefest of moments, I swear that his eyes flashed red and his mouth widened to reveal sharp pointed teeth, and then I blinked and Bubba was back to normal.

Whatever normal was.

"Your buddy scratched his finger," he winked. "A little blood sure goes a long way."

Documents signed, Stu slid his chair backwards, and as he stood up I caught a glimpse of a few red spots on and around the flamboyant scrawl of his signature.

Stu licked the tip of his finger as he replaced the cap on the fountain pen, returned it to Bubba and then turned, his shit-eating grin flashing wide as he spotted me. "I got it," he said. "I got Hank Williams' Cadillac."

Standing behind Stu, Bubba looked directly into my eyes, gave a smirk that almost made me shit my pants, and then picked up a sheaf of documents and a set of car keys and handed them to Stu.

Stu thanked him and then winked at me. "C'mon man," he said. "Let's get our stuff."

Putting his hand on my shoulder, Stu steered me out of the office, and once clear he leaned in close. "He's taking my Honda," he said. "Didn't even want to look at it." His eyes glittered. "My car, plus six-hundred bucks, and we're driving away in a Cadillac."

Stu's grin stretched wider. "He even took a check for the six hundred and said he's gonna fuel her up and she'll be ready by the time we get our stuff together."

I gave a half-hearted return to his fist-bump and followed him back towards his now previous car. My mind raced as I struggled to catch up with what had happened, words scrambling in my head as I attempted to give voice to the serious concern that I felt.

In the end the best I could come up with was a bad feeling that some heavy shit was about to go down.

Another shiver ran through me. I looked back over my shoulder, Bubba remained by the door of the office, his steel blue eyes locked onto me like a laser-sight.

I turned back and ran a little to catch up with Stu.   "What happened back there?" I said.

Stu sucked on his bleeding finger. "What do you mean?"

"How did you cut your finger?"

He thought for a moment. "You know? That was some weird shit. The dude gave me a fancy pen and as I took the cap off, something scratched my finger. It was like it hit an artery." He paused, and then grinned. "Bubba said he didn't expect me to sign it blood."

A spoonful of vomit hit the back of my mouth and then burned down my throat.

"What about before?" I said.

"What do you mean?"

"Well," I said. "When Bubba was showing you the car, he blocked me out and I heard him saying something, and…"

The words died on my lips. Saying them out loud made me feel stupid.

Stu shrugged. "After you walked away, we talked about the car. He said that it was meant for me, that I was meant to drive it." He grinned. "At first I thought it was pure salesman BS, but then I kinda believed him, the car IS meant for me. It all kinda makes sense."

"Sense?" I said. "We chance upon a car lot in Christ knows where, run by Colonel Sanders, who convinces you that you're meant to be driving a '52 Cadillac. Putting aside the matter of a fucking crow with a voice like throat cancer, in what dimension does any of this shit make any kind of sense?"

"Always with the negativity," said Stu. "But that's what I'm talking about. Bubba told me I deserve this car. With all the shit I've had to put up with, he said that it's only right that I get something back."

He put his hand on my shoulder. "It's all good, Bro'," he winked. "I got me a car, it's as big as a whale and we're about to set sail. Chill out, man, these are some righteous wheels, and we can road trip in style, now. Just think of the panties that are gonna drop when we roll into town driving this bad boy."

"Stu," I said. "Have you ever heard the phrase, 'if it sounds too good to be true, it probably is?'"

"No, I have not," he said. "Have you ever heard the phrase, 'my buddy is acting like a prissy little bitch because I secured the used-car deal of the century?'"

"The deal of a lifetime," rasped the crow.

Startled, both Stu and I spun around to see the crow observing us from the vantage point of Bubba's left shoulder.

Insanely, I wondered if the bird had ever shit down Bubba's back, and I had to bite my cheeks to quell hysterical laughter.

Ignoring me, Bubba smiled at Stu. "The Cadillac is good to go," he said. "Thought I'd come and help y'all with your bags."

A few minutes later we were heading out of the car lot. As we reached the exit, I saw Bubba start the Honda and drive it towards the entrance. Stu sounded the horn, gunned the engine, and gave a rebel yell as he swung the Caddie out onto the road, the big ol' car twerking on its springs before straightening, and then leaping forward with a V8 roar as Stu gave it the juice.

"Oh MAN, listen to that motor." Stu cupped his groin. "Yeah baby, we gonna get us some serious poon-TANG with this m'fucker. Know'm sayin?"

Now that we were driving away from Bubba I felt myself begin to relax.

"This is indeed," I said. "One righteous automobile."

It didn't take long to blow out of the other side of town, and soon we were out in the Texas desert, barreling down a nowhere road that was straighter than a preacher and longer than a memory. Apart from distant hills, there were no landmarks, road signs or any sign of life. Just an asphalt scar bisecting miles of Texas scrubland.

Stu frowned and began to shift in his seat. "Something's sticking in my ass," he said.

Just as I was about give an obvious reply, Stu leaned to one side, slid his hand into the back pocket of his jeans and produced the keys to the Honda.

For the second time that day we both said, "What the fuck?"

"I thought you only had one set of keys?" I said.

"I do," said Stu.

"Then how did Bubba start the Honda?"

"Not only that," said Stu. "How the fuck did he start the Honda? I mean, that engine was dead, man."

We drove on in silence, and then Stu said, "He must have had a master key or something, and maybe a car dealer's trick to get the engine going."

I could tell that Stu believed that about as much as I did, but in the absence of an explanation I gave a non-committal grunt. Better to leave it there.

After a few more miles of silence, Stu slapped the rim of the steering wheel. "Man, where the hell are we?"

I checked my phone. Still no service.

"Beats the hell outta me," I said. "Just gotta keep going that way, I guess."

"Anything on the radio?"

I shrugged, twisted the chrome knob on the radio, and shook my head at the static hissing from the speaker as I punched all the preset station buttons and wound the tuning needle from left to right and back again.

"Nope," I said.

I switched off the radio, and then idly ran my fingers along the chrome trim and across the walnut panel. As I pushed the latch on the glove compartment, the lid dropped down and a plastic object skittered towards me.

"What the hell's that?" said Stu.

I picked it up. "Looks like an eight-track," I said.

"Do what now?"

"An eight-track cartridge," I said. "Used to play music in the days before cassettes, CDs or iTunes."

"No shit? Who's on it?"

I turned the cartridge over, it was well-worn, the faded label barely legible. "Looks like a Hank Williams album," I said.

"Hank Williams, you say? Would that be THE Hank Williams? Erstwhile owner of this fine automobile? Defence rests, your Honor. Well, what are you waiting for? Put it on, my man."

Now, I could have sworn it wasn't there when we first got in the car, but beneath the dashboard hung a bulky Motorola eight-track cartridge player. Switching it and the radio on, I pushed the cartridge into the slot. The hissing ceased and the hypnotic pedal steel and rhythm guitar intro to 'Rambling Man' burst out of the speakers.

For three and a half minutes, Stu and I were entranced by Hank Williams' melancholic voice singing about how the sound of a freight train gives him itchy feet. The song finished, and after a brief pause, started again.

"Must be on repeat," said Stu. "Put it on shuffle, let's see what else is on there."

"It's a tape," I said. "It just plays, there's no shuffle. You can't even fast forward."

The song repeated three more times before we both had enough and I switched it off.

"Man, where ARE we?"

The road continued to stretch ahead of us, the landscape unchanged.

"You know," said Stu. "Since we left Rambling, we ain't seen no road signs, or buildings, or cars or people."

I was about to reply when in the distance, what looked like a small wooden cross, planted by the side of the road, came into view. As we drew closer, it became clear that the cross was the first of six signs, painted red with white lettering, spaced at intervals of about a hundred yards, and which, when read in sequence made up a message.

Six more miles/you took the bait/signed in blood/accept your fate/enjoy the ride/Burma Shave

"Burma Shave?" said Stu. "Like in the Tom Waits' song?"

"It was an old advertising campaign," I said. "For shaving cream. They used to put up signs just like that along the road. I wonder what 'six more miles' means?"

"To the graveyard," said Stu.

"What?"

"Six more miles to the graveyard, it's a Hank Williams song."

He paused. "And I signed in blood, what the fuck does that mean?"

I turned to Stu. "It probably means nothing," I said.

He pointed ahead. "There's some more signs."

The Cadillac slowed as we approached them, Stu reading the words.

Too late now/too late to weep/you are the company/that you keep/enjoy the ride/Burma Shave

"Man, this is fucked up."

"It's just some old saying," I said. "They probably used it because it scans across the signs."

"Maybe." Stu didn't sound convinced, or look any less scared.

"Holy shit."

Stu's eye's widened. I looked out of the windshield to see the horizon filled by a bank of black storm clouds that rolled and tumbled towards us, releasing a curtain of rain that drew steam from the hot asphalt.

The Caddie skidded to a halt. The torrential rain sounding like a standing ovation as it raced towards us. Stu stabbed a button and we heard the reassuring purr as the powered roof unfolded and closed over us just as the first fat raindrops hit the windshield and then pelted the roof with a sound like gravel pouring onto a tin roof.

Stu shook his head. "Where the fuck did this come from?"

"It's just a storm," I said. "It'll pass over us."

"That ain't just no storm," he said. "Look at the size of that mother-fucking cloud."

I'd never seen Stu spooked like that. I slid across the bench seat and put my arm around his trembling shoulders. "Take it easy, man, I said. "It's just a dumb old sign and a rainstorm. Hell, we're gonna be US Marines, bro. Two weeks into Boot Camp this is gonna seem like good times."

He seemed to calm down. "I guess," was all he said.

Stu put the Caddie in gear, and with the wipers barely keeping up with the onslaught of rain, we set off slowly along the road.

We drove in silence, and then I caught Stu staring intently at the dashboard.

"What's up?" I said.

"I'm watching the odometer," he said. "We're about two miles away."

"Away from where?"

Stu shrugged. "From whatever was six miles away from that sign."

Stu frowned, and then sniffed. "Eww, gross. Have you unloaded? That stinks."

I gagged as an unholy stench filled the car. "Dude," I said. "That was not me."

Rain hit the side of my face as I dropped the window to let in some air. It helped, but not much.

I felt the car slow and looked over at Stu. He had one hand holding his nose, his eyes lifting and dropping as he checked first the road ahead and then the odometer.

The Caddie pulled over and rolled to a halt.

"Why are you stopping?" I said.

"I'm not," said Stu. "The car's driving itself, look."

He stamped on the throttle, mashing it to the floor several times. It made no difference, the Caddie's engine idled briefly and then the glorious V8 rumble lapsed into silence.

"Way to go, Stuart," I said. "You broke two cars in one day."

Stu flipped the bird as rain continued to batter the car, the heavy clouds closing in, reducing visibility outside to only a few feet.

The stench grew stronger, now a foul taste soiling the back of my mouth. I gagged again, and then heard something move behind me. Stu heard it too, we both turned to look back and screamed in perfect unison with a thunderclap as a flash of lightning illuminated the body of a man slumped across the rear seat.

The man shuffled to sit upright; his features hidden in the shadow of a battered Stetson hat, his skeletal form draped in what looked like the tattered remains of an ornate country and western stage costume.

Another lightning flash obliterated the shadows. The man looked around and then leaned back into the seat as if to get comfortable. Pausing for a second, he crossed his legs, raised a finger and tipped the Stetson to reveal desiccated skin stretched over the prominent cheekbones of a once-handsome face now gaunt with decomposition.

A thousand miles away, I heard Stu scream again as the man scratched his thin, pointed nose, cleared his throat with a sound like a coffin lid being prised open, and then parted his thin lips in a macabre smile.

"Howdy boys," he said. "My name's Hank Williams. Now, which one of y'all bought my car?"

I choked back a gasp as the fetid breath carrying his words washed over me. Over the sound of the rain I heard a retch followed by liquid splatter and turned to see Stu leaning over the door like a seasick passenger, his body convulsing in a post-vomit shudder.

Hank Williams winked at me. "That can happen," he said. "Now start the car and drive about a hundred feet and turn into them gates up ahead."

I stared at Stu, and Stu stared at me until Hank Williams broke the spell.

"Well go on, goddamit," he said. "They'll all be here soon."

Stu's hand shook as he fumbled and then turned the key. The V8 rumble reintroducing a brief sense of normality as the Cadillac moved forwards.

I looked over my shoulder just in time to see Hank Williams press a finger against the side of his nose and snort a bloated maggot from his right nostril.

"Who-all's going to be here, sir?" My voice sounded small.

Hank Williams sniffed, paused, and then said, "The rest of 'em."

"Rest of who?" I said.

"All in good time, son," said Hank Williams. "All in good time."

I felt the Cadillac sway as it turned to the right, and then straightened to glide beneath a huge wrought-iron archway that stood at least twenty feet high, topped in large, ornate letters that spelled two words:

Rambling Cemetery

"Rambling?" I said, "We've been driving for like hours and we're still in Rambling? How big is this place?"

"Oh, Rambling ain't a place, son," said Hank Williams. "Not as such, you could say it's an existence, an actuality."

The rain stopped as we passed through the arch, the clouds rolling away into the distance and leaving behind a freshly scrubbed blue sky.

"Drop the hood, son," said Hank Williams. "Let's get us some fresh air around here."

Stu stopped the Cadillac, dropped the hood and then rolled forwards. The world was quiet save for the sound of the V8 and the crunch of tires on a tree-lined gravel track that stretched ahead for what looked like a quarter of a mile.

Hank Williams leaned forwards. "Up yonder, the track opens out to a big ol' circle. Like a lollipop on a stick. Imagine it's a clock and we're driving up from the six. I want y'all to park at the twelve, facing back this way. You got that, son?"

Stu nodded, his face ashen.

Hank Williams relaxed back into the seat until Stu finished manoeuvring and the car was pointed at the archway.

"Switch off the engine, son."

Stu turned the key and the Cadillac fell silent. In the back, Hank Williams hummed a tune that collapsed into a racking cough and ended with something being spat out of the car and hitting the gravel with a sound that will live with me forever.

"Here they come," said Hank Williams.

I looked up as a procession of automobiles turned into the cemetery and made their way slowly towards us, and it took me few seconds to realise that all the cars came from Bubba's car lot.

The old Packard led the way, driving counter-clockwise around the circle, stopping in front of us, and then reversing to park about ten feet to our right.

"Bessie Smith," mumbled Stu. "1937, on Highway 61, between Memphis, Tennessee and Clarksdale, Mississippi."

I looked sideways, Stu was slumped low against the back of the bench seat, and locked into a classic thousand-yard stare.

"You OK, buddy?" I said.

"James Dean," said Stu. "1955, Cholame, California."

"Do what now?"

"James Dean," he said. "Crashed at the junction of California State Route 46 (former 466) and California State Route 41."

I looked out just in time to see a Porsche 550 Spyder, reversing to park on the other side of the Packard.

After that came a 1966 Buick Electra, which reversed next to the Porsche.

"Jayne Mansfield," said Stu. "1967, Ringlet's Bridge, between New Orleans and Slidell, Louisiana."

Next to the Buick came a 1937 Cord Phaeton.

Slumped even lower in his seat, Stu stared at the steering wheel, his lower jaw slack, a pool of saliva building up behind his lip.

"Tom Mix," he said, saliva drooling down his chin. "1940, Highway 80, Arizona."

A 1950 Oldsmobile 88 pulled in.

Almost catatonic, Stu grunted, "Jackson Pollock. 1956, Springs, New York."

The final car was the midnight blue Lincoln convertible. As it too took its place, Stu's eyelids fluttered, his voice a faint whisper.

"November 29, 1963, Dallas, Texas. Hail to the Chief," he said.

"Time to go, boys," said Hank Williams, the Cadillac rocking gently as he climbed out.

"Go where?" I said.

Hank Williams walked around to the driver's door. "Well son," he said. "Things are gonna change, and we're a-gonna leave."

He placed his hand on Stu's shoulder. "And this'n, he's comin' with us."

I heard doors slamming and the scuffling of feet.

"He's not going anywhere," I shouted. "Get your fucking hands off of him."

"It's meant to be, son," said Hank Williams. "He signed in blood."

I lunged towards Stu, but a strong hand grabbed my arm and pulled me back. I looked up to see a man smiling down at me, he turned slightly as I tried to pull away and I saw that on the right side of his head was missing, the gaping hole revealing an empty brain cavity.

As I began to scream, the man smiled and then spoke with high-class Boston accent.

"It's meant to be, son," he said. "Time to say goodbye."

"Hail to the Chief," giggled Stu, as Hank Williams helped him out of the car.

"Leave him alone," I shouted. "Let him go."

"Your friend's going to be just fine," said the man. "It won't be long now."

He released his grip on my arm, and then turned to follow Hank Williams.

"It's meant to be, sugar." I turned to see a one-armed black lady wearing a floral dress and a cloche hat. She had a kindly smile as she took my hand. "You friend gotta go now," she said. "Like the fat man said, 'it is what it is, and it ain't no more'n that.'"

She also turned and walked towards Hank Williams, who had led Stu to the centre of the circle, quickly surrounded by the occupants of the vehicles.

The crow landed on the windshield, "Time to go," it rasped. "It's meant to be."

"Go fuck yourself," I said.

"Aww now, there's no need to be like that, son," Bubba appeared from nowhere, stood by the door and leaned into the Cadillac. "It ain't nothin' personal," he said. "Yo' friend gotta come with us, and you gotta go back."

"Back where?"

"From whence you came, son," he said. "From whence you came."

"What about Stu?"

"Like I said, he's comin' with us."

"To where?"

"To where we're going, which ain't for you to know."

He paused. "Things are gonna change, son. And you're gonna leave."

"I want to know where you're taking Stu," I said.

"We ain't takin' him nowhere. He comin' with us, on account of it's his time."

Bubba snapped his fingers.

The crow attacked before I had chance to react. I heard the flap of a wingbeat, felt talons rip at my flesh and then my eye erupted in a red mist. The noise was deafening, the crow screaming continuously as it attacked, and then lifted just out of reach before dive-bombing me again and again, from different directions and with a disorienting ferocity as it slashed, pecked and pummeled me.

I scrabbled for the door handle, fell out of the car, and grazed my hands as I scuttled across the gravel, stooping low as I tried to protect my head and neck from the frenzied aerial assault.

And then it stopped.

I heard a lonesome "screeee", and saw a golden eagle circling high above me.

For a second all was still, and then the crow came in fast from the left, hitting the side of my head like missile. As I tried to fight it off, I saw the eagle's wings fold and then I lost balance, tripped over and everything went black.

I don't know how long I was out but when I came to, the cemetery was empty. Staggering to my feet, I swayed a little before my head cleared and then took stock. All the cars were gone and no one was around. I was alone, the back of my hands were cut to ribbons, my face felt sore and I could taste blood in my mouth. A few feet away a large black feather, its quill stained with congealed blood, ruffled in the light breeze.

I began to walk, crunching footsteps into the gravel as I headed out of the cemetery. When I reached the archway, I turned right and continued walking. The sun was low over the horizon and my shadow lengthened as I tramped along the side of the road.

After about a mile or so I came upon another bunch of signs.

All things pass/all hardships end/respect the memory/of your friend/enjoy the ride/Burma Shave

At the side of the road, a golden eagle stood over a black, feathered carcass. As I approached, it lifted its wings, flexed a huge talon, gripped the remains of the crow and lifted majestically into the air. I watched it until it disappeared and then I turned and watched the sky catch fire as the sun kissed the horizon. Overwhelmed with exhaustion, I lay down beneath the Burma Shave sign.

*****

I woke up hooked up to a machine in a hospital just outside Amarillo. The first thing the nurse told me was that I'd been in a coma for six week.

The second thing she told me was that Stu was dead. Apparently we were going at better 'n eighty miles an hour when the Honda blew a tire. An eyewitness said the car rolled about a dozen times before it left the road. Stu died instantly, and I'm told it took firefighters an hour to cut me out of the wreckage. They said the crash had shut the interstate for a whole day and made the TV news.

I was in hospital for another two weeks. On the day of my discharge, "One-eyed Joe" turned up to fetch me. Turns out, he'd phoned around all

279

the hospitals in the area, and then called every day to check how I was.

When I thanked him, he smiled gently. "Semper Fi," he whispered.

As we drove back in his old Chevy pick-up, two good eyes between us, Joe told me that on the day it happened, he'd seen us in a dream and had woken up to find himself gripping the remains of a dead crow.

Said his fingers were locked with cramp.

Said they hurt for days.

Said he's been sober ever since.

I have no memory of the crash, and while I refuse to think about, or imagine the manner of his death, Stu is never far away from my thoughts. In my version of events he's still somewhere out there, driving the back-roads of Texas, the hood down, wearing fake Oakley wraparounds, bopping his fingers on the steering wheel of Hank Williams' Cadillac.

Rain Dogs

*This story first appeared in **Mix Tape Volume 1**, a collection of stories inspired by song titles, and published by Burdizzo Books.*

Are you sitting comfortably?

Then I'll begin.

Once upon a time, in a tumbledown cottage in a field in the Gloucestershire countryside there lived a middle-aged couple called Joan and Bob.

A lifetime of indolence and a fondness for the wrong types of food had crafted Joan's physique into a shape that Bob, in his braver moments, likened to a furious, female version of Penfold from Danger Mouse.

Of course, he never said that out loud, because it would propel Joan into a seething, spitting, cursing rage, as many things often did.

Bob was of slight build, with a mousy comb-over that was turning grey. A quiet, ineffectual man, he bore Joan's frequent wrathful outbursts with apparent fortitude. He would never react, or shout back, which would infuriate Joan, who would then escalate into a screaming fit that could be heard three fields away by their neighbour (a farmer who kept prize sheep).

Thirty years previously, when they bought their tumbledown cottage, it was an idyllic country home with views to die for.

One morning, not long after they first moved in, Joan asked Bob if he could put up some bookshelves. Bob said that he would do it that very evening, if Joan could tidy the room up a little so that it was ready for him to start when he came home from work.

Joan's apoplexy that day went into the record books, for length, content and originality. Spittle flew from her lips as she screeched invectives that questioned Bob's parentage, the size of his genitals, his physique and his general usefulness to mankind. The summary of this diatribe was Joan's assertion that it wasn't her effing job to clean the effing house.

Bob replied calmly that in that case, it wasn't his effing job to put up the effing bookshelves. Neither would budge from their position and there then followed a thirty-year Mexican standoff during which neither of them made any effort to clean or maintain the house ever again.

Nowadays, the views were the same but their tumbledown cottage was a shithole. A stinking, festering, dilapidated shithole.

Every room was piled high with cardboard boxes, bin-liners, books, clothes, magazines and newspapers, all coated in a thick layer of dust. The only visible floor space was a pathway of cracked and worn linoleum that connected the filthy, defeated, dog-hair-covered armchairs in front of the TV to the equally filthy and defeated kitchen; in which grease-stained work surfaces supported unwieldy towers of dirty crockery. Congealing food waste covered the floor and rats lived in the cupboard under the sink.

Bob couldn't remember the last time they'd had visitors.

Joan and Bob also kept dogs. Six large German Shepherds who lived in cramped wire cages stacked in the corner of the living room. The cages were lined with months-old newspapers that were stiff with dried urine and dog slobber, all of which contributed to the overall aroma of the house.

When friends used to ask how they could live in such chaos, Joan's mouth would tighten with prim sanctimony.

"I have better things to do," she would say. "And besides, tidy people don't make the same exciting discoveries that I do."

"Tidy people don't live in stinking squalor," thought Bob.

But of course, he never said that out loud.

Joan didn't have a job. Instead she preferred to sit at home all day, either reading cheap paperbacks (25p for 10 from a charity shop) or at the keyboard of her ancient PC, dispensing her advanced internet-wisdom (Joan was NEVER wrong) among internet forums, chat-rooms or Facebook groups.

In the parlance of Oscar Wilde, Joan knew the price of everything and the value of nothing. An avid frequenter of charity shops, she particularly enjoyed browbeating the hapless staff (usually elderly volunteer workers) to "get a better deal". Her favourite story was the time she bullied a 75-year-old retired teacher (a smiling, sweet-natured, grey haired old lady) into slashing £1.50 off the price of a manky leather handbag, which was marked up at three pounds. The ferocity of Joan's malice, intimidation and general nastiness that day was such that the elderly lady gave up volunteering, developed acute social anxiety and never set foot out of her house until twelve months later when she was taken into care suffering from early-onset senile dementia.

When Joan returned home victorious she threw the handbag on top of the pile of rubbish in the back bedroom, never to be touched again.

"It was a bargain," she declared. "That's how I roll."

Like all sociopathic bullies, Joan was particularly fond of attacking anyone who was unable to fight back. Years ago, when Joan and Bob used to socialise, restaurant waiting staff were her targets of choice. Joan would often boast about reducing a waitress to tears with a foul-mouthed diatribe regarding some non-existent food complaint in order to get a couple of pounds knocked off the bill.

All that ended when they stopped going out to restaurants. Friends drifted away because of Joan's behaviour towards them. She would be openly critical, firing off cruel, spiteful and sarcastic barbs with the intention of inflicting the maximum amount of hurt and upset. If anyone tried to counter Joan, or criticise her in any way, she would rant about it for weeks, every slight stored away in her elephantine memory of grudges, and relived time and again through internal dialogues which would end with Joan crushing her foe with a vicious verbal slap-down.

Very soon, Joan and Bob had no friends.

"People don't like me," she would declare. "Because I tell it like it is."

"People don't like you," thought Bob. "Because you're a spiteful, loudmouthed bully."

But of course, he never said that out loud.

Bob was a travelling salesman. He knew his stuff, and away from Joan he was a different person, animated, articulate, charming and persuasive. His patch covered the whole of the UK and he would often spend long days on the road.

When he got home, often late at night, it was his effing job (according to Joan) to let the German Shepherds out into the muddy, dog-shit-ridden wasteland that in days-gone-by had been a thriving vegetable patch. After that he would sit in front of the TV with a large tumbler of cheap blended whisky (supermarket own-brand, in a plastic bottle. Bob still shuddered at the memory of Joan completely losing her shit in the middle of a busy Tesco Express when he'd had the temerity to pick up a bottle of single-malt).

Bob liked watching DVDs of Formula One highlights. If he didn't fall asleep in the chair (which most nights he did), he would climb into bed next to Joan, and lie awake listening to her snoring as he tried to remember why he married her in the first place.

One day, Bob was with a client in Cumbria. It had been a long day. He'd managed to secure a very lucrative deal but it was late afternoon before he was able to get away. At first, he planned to go straight home, but the radio warned of a band of gales, thunderstorms and torrential rain, which was forecast to sweep the country. Furthermore, local traffic news told Bob that the M6 Southbound was closed due to an accident near Preston. Bob made a rare decision, pulled into a service station and booked a room at the Travelodge.

Bob rang Joan to tell her that he wasn't going to be home that night, and that he had another site visit in Nottingham the next day, but assured her that he should be home about teatime.

Joan snorted her disinterest. "What-effing-ever," she said. "As long as you're here to let the effing dogs out."

Bob said that he would see her tomorrow.

"Eff off and die," snarled Joan as she slammed the phone down.

The next day, driving conditions were horrendous. At the Manchester bottleneck the traffic on the M6, hampered by driving rain, spray, reduced visibility and several accidents, had slowed to a crawl. Bob rang to cancel the appointment with the client, and then called home. Joan didn't answer and so Bob left a message telling her that he might be late, but would be home as soon as he could.

Eleven hours later, Bob was three miles from home, driving along a single-track country lane. The storm had worsened, battering the car in a deluge of rain that the windscreen wipers had no hope of clearing. Tired and disoriented, Bob came around a bend just a little too fast, failed to register the flood marker and ploughed into four feet of standing water.

The engine died with a bang. The electrics expired soon after.

In pitch darkness Bob fumbled into the glove compartment, pulled out a large torch and emergency hammer, and then grabbed his waterproof jacket from the back seat. As he contorted into the jacket, rainwater cascaded from the surrounding fields, pushing the flood higher around the car until the bonnet was awash.

It took several blows with the hammer to smash the sunroof glass and Bob was breathing hard when he eventually clambered onto the roof. Kneeling down, crouched against the wind, Bob switched on the torch and then gasped. The flood stretched for at least fifty yards in front of the car and was rising fast to cover the road behind. The torch revealed that the grass verges on either side were still just above the waterline. Bob got to his feet, steadied himself against the wind, took a deep breath and jumped.

He almost made it.

Landing on the grass verge, Bob grabbed the hedge and then howled in pain as a large thorn impaled itself deep into the palm of his hand. Jerking his hand away, he lost balance and fell backwards into the flood. Hitting the side of the car kept Bob on his feet, but the shock of the sudden chest-deep immersion in freezing water forced the air out of his lungs in a single explosive gasp. Lightheaded, frightened and panting, Bob panic-splashed his way to the rear of the car and managed to wade clear of the flood and back onto the road.

When he'd calmed down, he forced his hand into a sodden pocket and retrieved his phone. It was waterlogged and useless. After a few moments of taking stock, Bob thought he knew where he was and planned a route home across the fields.

Backtracking along the lane, Bob found a metal farm gate, grabbed the top and howled again as his thorn-damaged hand gripped the rusty barbed-wire wrapped around the top bar. Cursing as he straddled the gate, he cried out again as his foot slipped, and as he pitched headfirst into a patch of mud and cow shit he felt the barbed wire slash deep into his trailing leg. The field was on the side of a steep hill, at the top of which was a footpath which would lead eventually to the tumbledown cottage.

As Bob scrambled to his feet the field lit up with a brilliant phosphorescent glow, followed by an explosion of thunder directly overhead. Following his torch light, Bob set off up the hill.

Almost cresting the hill, Bob was fifty feet downstream of hundred-year-old oak tree, around which a torrent of surface water poured down the field. As Bob's foot splashed into the water, a lightning bolt hit the oak tree and arced along the stream. Bob saw the flash, felt the punch of a steam hammer and then everything went black.

When he regained consciousness, Bob found himself lying face-down in cow shit. His joints ached with every movement, his teeth hurt and the stench of scorched hair filled his nostrils.

He finally arrived home three hours later, drenched, bleeding, caked in mud and shivering violently.

As he searched for his door key, Bob could see Joan bathed in the glow of her computer screen, her face distorted by the rain on the outside of the window and the thick layer of grime on the inside. Bob tapped on the glass. Joan looked up, mouthed an invective and then returned to the screen. Eventually Bob found his door key and let himself in, the familiar wall of stench hitting him in the face.

"Where the eff have you been?

"I drove into a flood," said Bob. "I had to walk back across the fields. I was struck by lightning."

"Teatime, you said."

"No, I called you after that," said Bob. "I left a message on the answerphone."

"I didn't get any effing message."

Bob looked over to the base station of their cordless telephone, where a large, green, '1' flashed brightly in the gloom of the cottage.

"I gave your dinner to the dogs," said Joan.

Bob felt his pulse twitching in his temple.

"Did you renew my car insurance?" he said.

"What?" Joan didn't look up.

"My car insurance," said Bob. "You said you would ring them up and get it renewed."

Joan shrugged. "I don't think I did."

"I gave you the renewal letter," said Bob. "I asked you to call the insurance company and get it renewed."

Joan stared fixedly at the computer screen. "It's not my effing job," she said. "To follow you around wiping your arse for you."

"The car's waterlogged," said Bob. "The engine's fucked. If it's not insured we're stuffed."

Joan shrugged again.

"Not my problem," she said.

A nerve twitched beneath Bob's left eye. "I'm freezing," he said. "I need a shower."

The bathroom was toxic. A thick, grey, tidemark ringed the inside of the cracked, plastic avocado bath, above which black mould was spreading up the damp wall with ceiling ambitions. The floor mat around the toilet hadn't been lifted in years and was crusty with all manner of bodily excretions. The toilet itself looked like someone had filled a shotgun cartridge full of shit and fired it into the pan. Bob pressed the flush lever with his foot, closed the pan lid, wrestled himself out of his sodden clothes, and then stepped into the shower.

Half an hour later, dressed in pyjamas and wrapped up in a thick tartan dressing gown, Bob sat down in front of the TV, opened a new bottle of whisky, and filled the glass tumbler as he pressed play on the DVD remote.

He woke with a start in the early hours. The whisky bottle was empty, but his head felt surprisingly clear. Bob stood up, switched off the TV, and then went upstairs. Not bothering to get undressed, he lay on top of the bed and fell asleep to the sound of Joan snoring and the rain battering the windows.

At 3:30 am, Joan shook Bob awake. "I heard a noise in the kitchen," she said. "It might be a burglar. Go and check."

Bob doubted that any self-respecting burglar would be out in this weather, and even if they were he didn't think that they would stay very long in this stinking shithole of a house. Much less root through the kitchen.

But of course he never said that out loud.

Next to the bed, propped against the damp, mould-stained wall stood a baseball bat. It was heavy, made from hickory and had the words 'Louisville Slugger' burned into it. Bob had bought it the last time they visited America in September

2001. He remembered Joan kicking off at the airport staff because their flight home had been cancelled due to the attacks on the Twin Towers. Joan had spent the rest of the day pointing and sneering at weeping Americans.

Bob picked up the bat, made his way downstairs and paused to listen.

The house was quiet.

Bob stepped softly towards the kitchen, pushed the door open and switched on the light. A six-foot rat was sitting upright on a chair, leaning on the table and gnawing on a three-week-old chicken leg.

The rat looked up.

"Hey Bob," said the rat. "You and I need to have a little talk. Why don't you let the dogs out and then pull up a chair."

A wall of rain hit Bob as he opened the front door, the dogs almost knocking him over as they bolted into the darkness.

Bob returned to the kitchen, sat down and soon he and the rat were putting the world to rights.

When the police arrived they found the front door wide open, and Bob in the kitchen sitting at the table talking to an empty chair and gnawing on a half-eaten rat. He was covered in blood and spattered with brains and other human matter.

They found Joan in the bedroom, her head beaten to a pizza-like mush from which a lake of blood had spread across the floor like a cartoon speech bubble. Next to her, the baseball bat lay broken in two, its splintered end matted with blood, hair and brains. Joan was formally identified by her teeth, some of which were embedded in the bat, the rest scattered across the room.

The coroner called it a vicious and sustained attack.

The police had been called by the neighbouring sheep farmer, who had woken up to the sounds of animals in distress. When he reached the field, the farmer dropped to his knees. His entire flock was dead. Savaged by Joan and Bob's German Shepherds, who were now feasting on the carcasses.

The farmer went back into his house and returned with his shotgun and a leather bandolier filled with cartridges. He shot all six dogs and then called the police, sobbing uncontrollably as he tried to explain what had happened.

Bob was found guilty of the murder of his wife, and was sent to Broadmoor Psychiatric Hospital. He has a room to himself, which he keeps spotless.

Bob is the model inmate, and hopes that he never has to leave Broadmoor. It's the best place he's ever been and if he's ever released then he has decided that he will probably go out and kill some more people, just so that he gets sent back.

Bob says that out loud, at least twice a day. And because of that he lived happily ever after.

First Love

A tale of obsession.

I can't believe that I've found it.

I mean, I haven't been searching all that long but it's been on my mind for, well, let's see, 1979, that waaaaaas...bloody hell, thirty-four years.

Good God, has it really been that long?

Time flies like knives, they say.

And fruit flies like bananas.

Hah. Sorry, just a little play on words; one of my ways of getting through the day.

Funny where you find yourself, isn't it? If you'd told me in 1979 where I'd be right now I probably wouldn't have believed you. Then again, I didn't believe much of anything back then. Certainly didn't believe in myself.

That took a long time to happen.

Thirty-four years. You think you've got all the time in the world and then one day you look up and you're staring down the barrel at fifty and it hits you like a steam train that unless you're one of a select few, then you've lived for more years than you have remaining and all of a sudden you notice the clock is ticking faster and that you seem to be eating breakfast every ten minutes.

Still, I'm lucky enough to be in the position to have a complete change of lifestyle soon. I'll have a lot more time on my hands and be able to do all the stuff I've dreamed of doing.

It's now or never.

Elvis said that. In 1979 he'd been dead for two years. Shuffled off this mortal coil from the comfort of his crapper in Graceland. He was forty-two. As the song goes, enjoy yourself, it's later than you think.

Just ease up on the burgers.

Sorry, I have a tendency to ramble these days; jumping from thought to thought like a steel ball in a pinball machine. Do they still have pinball machines? I suppose it's all computer games now. Must check that out on Google.

To a seventies kid, the internet is amazing.

Sometimes I think the inside of my head is a bit like the internet, millions of hyperlinks cross-linked to billions of web-pages chronicling various life experiences.

Music usually kicks it off. Hearing a song, pretty much any song from the seventies really, is the aural equivalent of typing in the box and hitting 'Search'. Most songs will bring up at least a dozen pages of memories, each one different and each one linked to a dozen more. I can spend an entire day browsing there. Or is it surfing?

The internet inside my head helps me search through the past. The real internet is helping me search for a better future.

Everything comes to he who waits and Tom Waits said, "The large print giveth and the small print taketh away."

Sorry, rambling again.

Where was I? Ah yes, my triumphant discovery.

Thirty-four years.

At first, with the right amount of distraction - not to mention regular ingestion of mind-altering substances - I would go for months, years almost and not think about it once.

After I stopped taking the drugs, it began as an occasional thought every few weeks. An idle moment spent mulling things over might spark a memory which would lead to one of those 'I wonder...'' trains of thought, which I would follow for a short while before distraction kicked in.

Ever since I've been clean, thoughts and memories of my childhood have been flooding back.

It's probably an age thing. You know, more years behind than in front so why not focus on those that have gone past? Keep sifting through them enough and you'd be surprised at the treasures that come to the surface.

One or two kept popping up and then one in particular sparked the idea that began the search that may well shape my future.

I thought it would have taken much longer, but thanks to Facebook and even Friends Reunited - there's still a wealth of information on there - it was a piece of cake. You'd be surprised at the clues people leave lying around.

I still can't believe that I've actually found it.

The home address of my first love.

She was the first girl that I ever kissed and when I close my eyes I can replay that kiss over and over again. I can still feel her soft lips, savour the exquisite intimacy of her tongue against mine, smell her perfume mixed with the floor-polish odour of the school gymnasium. Holding her in my arms as the glitterball showered us with light-confetti to 'How deep is your love?' by The Bee-Gees. My first school disco, my first dance, my first kiss.

The intensity of the moment affected us both, I know it did.

Next day I asked her if she wanted to go out with me. Her friends sniggered when she turned me down. She told me that she'd drunk half a bottle of Strongbow before the disco and she'd only kissed me for a dare.

I remember my face burning as I walked away.

I can see now that she was acting up in front of them. No way was she going to admit to the

303

feelings that we had for one another, not in front of her friends.

We are both more mature now, able to deal with this as adults.

From next week my days will be my own again. I really can't wait. I'll dress up smart, get a massive bouquet of flowers and a box of chocolates and then turn up on her doorstep.

She'll open the door, gasp and put her hand to her mouth in surprise as I hand over the flowers and chocolates. Then she will blush as I ask her if she would like to go out to dinner that evening.

Of course, if she says no, I'll cut off her head.

Like I did to her mother in 1979.

Boozy Afternoon

Al Fresco dozing

in a white wine drowsy

Summer garden reverie

Lulled towards sleep

By distant skylark song

and soporific insect drone

Next to me you lie

Eyes closed

Sun kissed skin

like rose blushed porcelain

A bumble bee

With torpid buzz

Hovers above you as if in homage

To your timeless beauty

Dreamily you open reluctant

sleep heavy eyes

And then all fucking hell breaks loose

Two Turtle Doves

*A story of rock 'n' roll retribution that first appeared in **12 Days of Christmas**, a collection of horror stories with a Christmas theme, published by Burdizzo Books.*

My first guitar saved my life.

And I wish now that I'd never set eyes on it.

It was back in 1973.

I was on my way to step out in front of an express train. I knew a place where it would pass at full speed and I could walk onto the track at the very last second, giving the driver no time to brake.

I had it all planned.

See, when you're a skinny, underdeveloped, bespectacled, thirteen-year-old, stammering ginger bookworm with bad skin and acute social-anxiety, you become the target of choice for every thug, wanker and bullying dickhead looking for a docile recipient for their anger issues.

Dave Scott was Dickhead-in-Chief, with Alex, his twin brother, a very able lieutenant. They were two years older than me, and their joint mission in life was to hunt me down and kick the living shit out of me at every given opportunity. This they did often, and with an amount of pleasure, imagination and attention to detail that was terrifying.

Not that I was a stranger to the dark side of life. I had a brother in the army. He was my hero, hard as nails he was. But he was killed in Northern Ireland, which caused my dad to drink himself to death, leaving me and my mum on to struggle through life as best we could. Victims don't attract friends, and with no one to turn to, I lived in my head. It was, and still is, a dark and wretched place.

Welcome to my world. Welcome to my story.

When you're the victim of a bully your mind takes you to places where rules don't exist. Alone with your thoughts, a maelstrom of anger fuels your imagination such that in your head you create ever more violent acts of retribution. You feel your fists clench and your face contort as you fantasise about revenge; a hammer to the temple, a knife to the throat, a knitting needle pushed slowly into the ear, a razor blade dragged across an eyeball, bending a finger back until it snaps with a loud crack. Dreaming up a witty one-liner with each kick to their bollocks. Make them scream, make them bleed, make them hurt, make them beg for mercy. Taunt them. Humiliate them. Debase them. In your mind you're ready for them.

Until the next time. When you turn the corner, and you see them waiting, and you literally piss yourself with fear because you haven't got a hammer, or a knitting needle, or a knife, or the muscle, expertise or bravery to fight back, and you know damn well that very soon it will be you begging for mercy.

And the more that happens, the louder the voice in your mind tells you that you're worthless, and with no case for the defence you reach the point where the only way out is to make an appointment for a meeting with the business end of a speeding locomotive.

I was on my way to that meeting when I spotted the guitar propped up next to some dustbins outside the Oxfam shop in the High Street.

Up until that point I had never seen any kind of guitar up close, much less had any desire to learn to play one. This one was a cheap, wooden acoustic with nylon strings and plastic tuning pegs. I picked it up, ran my fingers across the strings, and something about the sound it made temporarily distracted me from the dark side of my brain.

There's a first time for everything, and there would be another express train tomorrow.

I took the guitar home, borrowed a couple of tuition books from the library, and set about devouring every spare minute to practicing. In a very short time I reached the point where I needed a better guitar.

Back then, Mum bought everything from a Mail Order catalogue, each week was a gamble as to whether we could scrape together enough to make the minimum payment.

Our neighbor, next door-but-one, was a representative, and Mum had borrowed a copy from her and left it on the kitchen table. I was flipping through it one evening when I found the "Musical Instruments" page.

That's when I saw it. The object of my dreams and the cause of future nightmares.

"El Diablo" was a cheap Chinese copy of a Gibson SG electric guitar. It had accentuated double-cutaways, and when you held it upright they resembled the horns of the devil. The body was painted in a red so vivid that it reminded me of a stab wound and branded the outline of Satan's head behind my eyelids every time that I blinked.

I spent over an hour staring at it (I even took a Polaroid photograph of the page, which I carried everywhere), a dark obsession growing inside me like a tumor as I pored over the technical specifications whilst ignoring the reality.

The price was an eye-watering £250. Even at the lowest weekly payment, spread over three years it was beyond my meagre budget. Asking mum for help was out of the question. We didn't have pot to piss in, and an electric guitar was right at the very bottom of a very long priority list.

That night I dreamt of it. And in my dream, I stood centre-stage in a dark, stinking dive-bar, playing to a crowd of slavering, writhing and fornicating scarlet demons. Demons that worshipped me as El Diablo screamed out a blistering, elongated siren call laden with reverb and feedback.

As I played, the room began to shudder, the dirt floor erupting ripe mud pustules through which corpses in various stages of decomposition scrabbled from their graves, stood upright, and then got their bad selves on down to the hellish groove. El Diablo screamed louder still, and then dive-bombed to a heavy, low-down 12-bar blues riff. Demons grunted like rutting pigs, shitting everywhere as the guttural power chords and driving bass line resonated deep within their bowels.

In the midst of this rancid, rocking, satanic hell-hole, one of the demons separated itself from the undulating mass, turned and lumbered towards me, its breath inundating my world with unholy stench as it morphed into Keith Richards.

312

"You get that axe, it's gonna change your life, man," Keith growled. "How much of a deposit would you need to afford the payments?"

Another corpse shuffled across the stage, strips of rotting material flapping and dangling from its bones, wisps of dirty grey hair creeping from beneath the rim of a filthy top hat. As it drew closer, scraps of desiccated facial muscle twitched in an obscene representation of a grin as the corpse laid its bony hand on my shoulder.

"Today is Friday," it hoarsed. "People always pay their bills on a Friday."

I erupted gasping from the nightmare, my pyjamas and bedclothes wringing with sweat, my heart thumping as I switched on the light and waited for the demonic images to fade.

The catalogue was on the floor where I'd left it. The photograph of El Diablo wiggling her curves at me, looking every bit as seductive as a Playboy magazine centre-fold.

At the back of the catalogue was about ten pages of small print. I speed-read through to the payment terms and worked out that a 20% deposit would halve the weekly payments over three years. Putting El Diablo well within my limited means.

All I had to do was find fifty pounds.

*****

It was dark when my alarm went off, and freezing cold when I slipped out of bed. Outside, the clear sky glistened with stars, the ground with frost and icy treachery.

I was halfway along my paper round when from behind I heard the familiar clinking bottles and low whirring electric hum of Sid Davies' milk float.

Sid gave a cheery wave as he drove past and then steered across the road to stop outside a block of flats.

I watched him step out of the cab, and reach for a crate of milk bottles.

I watched him heft the crate onto his shoulder, and then turn towards the flats.

I watched him take three steps, and then his feet shot from under him.

I saw his head hit the pavement, and from twenty feet away I heard his skull crack through the crash of breaking glass.

When I reached him, Sid wasn't moving. Blood poured from his ears, running along the camber of the pavement, mixing with the spilt milk to create a grotesque strawberry milkshake pooling in the gutter.

I remembered my brother telling me that if someone is bleeding from the ears, then it's not a good sign.

I knelt down and felt Sid's neck for a pulse like my brother had shown me.

Nothing.

I grabbed his wrist.

Nothing.

Sid always wore a battered leather satchel on a thin strap slung over his left shoulder. The satchel lay to one side, the flap was open and in the weak pool of sodium light I could see banknotes inside. Lots and lots of banknotes.

"It's Friday. Everyone pays their bills on a Friday."

"You get that axe, man, it's gonna change your life."

I looked up and down the street. It was still too early for signs of any movement. No lights coming on. No curtains twitching. No one around.

I looked back at Sid. Once more I checked his neck and his wrist for a pulse.

Nothing.

I checked the street again. All clear. My heart pounded as I slipped my hand inside the satchel, grabbed fistfuls of notes and stuffed them frantically into my paper sack.

"Whu…whu…whu…"

My body twitched and I stifled a scream as a hand grabbed my wrist. Sid was awake, staring up to the sky, gripping my arm, his cheeks puffing and deflating as he blew strange words into the cold morning air.

I leaned over him. "Can you hear me, Sid?"

"Whu…whu…whu…"

"Do you know who I am, Sid?"

"Whu…whu…whu…"

His left foot began to quiver, and then his leg shuddered violently.

"Sid?"

By now his head lay in a lake of blood, his eyes staring wildly. I pried his fingers from my wrist.

"Do you know where you are, Sid?"

"Whu…whu…whu…"

I looked around. The street was empty. Still no sign of anyone.

El Diablo flashed into my vision. Its body pulsing like arterial blood.

"You get that axe, man, it's gonna change your life."

I took a deep breath, grabbed Sid's head in both hands, lifted it and then with all my strength hammered it onto the pavement.

I felt something give, like the shattering of an eggshell.

"Whuwhuwhuwhu."

Sid's breathing became ragged.

I lifted his head again. Took a deep breath and began smashing it down with all the force I could muster. Again and again and again.

Crack.

Crack.

Crack.

Sid's eyeballs rolled upwards, his throat gave a final clattering gasp, and then he fell silent.

I smashed his head once more, saw something ooze from the back of his skull.

By now I was panting, my body sweating, my arms aching.

I stood up and looked around again. Still nobody about.

I stepped over Sid's body and carried on with my paper round. When I was out of sight from the street I started pulling banknotes out of my sack and stuffing them into my pockets.

Nobody saw me walking away.

Back at home, I laid the cash out on my bed.

One hundred and twenty-five pounds.

*****

Fast Forward to 1975.

By now I had learned some chops and my playing was getting pretty tasty. I was still underweight, still stammering, still short-sighted, still anxious and still ginger. But I could play the guitar just like ringing a bell.

Hours and hours and hours of finger-shredding practice, night after night was finally beginning to pay off. I could play pretty much anything, any style. I had inherited my brother's record collection and developed a preference for early electric blues, and listened to everything by the Rolling Stones up to Exile on Main St. (the last album he bought before the IRA blew him up).

The bullying had lessened somewhat. Encounters were fewer, but no less violent. Going out was safer, but the effects of my anxiety lingered on and my mind was still feeding me dark and sinister thoughts.

El Diablo was my comfort blanket, soaking up most of my anger, calming most of my fears and converting most of my bleak thoughts into sweet tones. Whatever mood I was in, she made me sound good, and when I thought the voices in my head weren't listening, I would daydream of a playing in a band and becoming a rock and roll hero.

The Turtle Doves were formed at my school in your standard rock group formation: lead singer, two guitarists, bassist and drummer.

Mick Taylor, the lead singer was a tall, skinny narcissist who thought he was Mick Jagger. He really wasn't.

Dave Scott was the original lead guitarist. The very same spiteful, loudmouth bastard bully who had made my formative years a living hell.

Rhythm guitarist was Alex Scott, Dave's twin brother and partner in crime.

Bassist was Jimmy Morton. Dedicated to music. Later on, Jimmy co-wrote all the songs with me.

The drummer was Tom Cornwell. Tom was a legend.

I'd watched them practice a few times at school, and soon noticed that cracks were beginning to appear. Jimmy wanted the band to record original material (he was a prolific songwriter), whereas Dave and Alex insisted on playing covers because they couldn't be arsed to put in the work to learn new chords and create something new. No one else in the band could write music and so Jimmy was outvoted every time. After one particularly memorable argument, the practice session ended with the Scott brothers storming off.

I walked out of school that afternoon to find both of them leaning against a wall, passing a cigarette back and forth. Dave's face twisted into a sneer.

"What are you looking at, you scrawny little cunt?"

"Nothing," I said. "Leave me alone."

I didn't see the first punch, just felt the explosion on my face and the familiar taste of blood in my mouth. The second punch put me on the ground, my head bouncing off the asphalt. After that, all I could do was curl up tight and try and protect myself against the volley of well-aimed kicks from Dave and his bastard brother.

I heard someone shouting, and then a scuffle, and then the kicking stopped and I was being lifted to my feet.

"Four-eyed ginger twat." The Scott brothers laughed as they swaggered away.

"Are you alright?" Jimmy looked genuinely concerned.

I sniffed back tears of humiliation. "I th-think so."

"Pair of wankers," said Jimmy.

He stepped back. "I've seen you watching us practice," he said. "You like music?"

I nodded. "I p-play guitar," I said. "Mostly b-blues-rock."

I showed him the latest Polaroid of El Diablo.

"That's a nice guitar," said Jimmy. "I bet it sounds amazing. Listen. We're playing at the Rose and Lion pub on Saturday night, why don't you come along? I'll make sure those two wankers won't bother you. Maybe we can hear you play?"

"M-maybe," I said. "Thanks."

"See you on Saturday, then." Jimmy turned and walked away.

When he'd gone I stared for a long time at the picture.

By now the Polaroid was about six months old, the glossy paper well-worn and creased, the image beginning to fade. But as I stared at the picture the colour of El Diablo seemed to become more vivid.

"Burning like the flames of hell."

The voice made me jump. Its sinister tone suggesting another kicking was inbound, but when I looked around there was no one there.

*****

The Rose and Lion was a down-at-heel pub in a shabby side street that led to a small park and kids' playground.

The gig didn't go well. Early on, a burly, shaven-headed punter made his way to the stage and began to heckle Dave loudly. At first Dave tried to ignore him, but the shaven-headed guy was relentless and seemed to know which buttons to press.

He kept on heckling until Dave stopped playing, grabbed his guitar by the neck and hit the floor swinging. Punches were traded, Dave was pulled away, and Shaven-Headed Guy was bundled out of the pub. The gig never recovered and I went home soon after.

The next morning Jimmy turned up at my place.

"We're looking for a new guitarist," he said. "It looks like Dave's gonna be out of action for a long time. You interested?"

Jimmy told me that after leaving the pub, the Shaven-Headed Guy hung around outside. Later that night, witnesses saw him grab Dave and frog march him into the park.

Next morning, Dave was found unconscious near the swings. Every single bone in his body had been systematically and expertly broken.

A couple of weeks later, on a Friday afternoon, I went to visit Dave in hospital. He was out of Intensive Care and in a room on his own. Encased in a body cast, and hanging from traction wires, he looked like a wounded marionette.

I walked up to the bed and leaned in close. The bruising on his face had ripened to a midnight blue, with patchy clouds of sickly yellow. His broken jaw was wired shut, rendering his trapped words unintelligible.

"Not so scary now, are you? You fucking wanker."

Swollen, bloodshot eyes stared back at me, first with contempt, then uncertainty, and then widening in fear as I licked his face, dragging my tongue from his chin to his forehead.

I leaned closer, to whisper in his ear.

"Take a good look, because my face is the last thing you're ever going to see. I hope you burn in hell, you piece of shit."

I grabbed a pillow from an armchair next to the bed, placed it over Dave's face and pushed down hard.

It was over in seconds. The bed shook violently at first, and then calmed, and then silence.

I looked up at the sound the scratch-flare of a match, and the smell of burning tobacco.

Sid, the milkman, stood in the corner of the room, dragging on a Woodbine. His pallid, death-mask creased into a grin as cigarette smoke poured from his nostrils and mouth.

"It's Friday," he said. "People always pay their bills on a Friday."

Sid winked at me. "You did a good job with me," he said. "When they lifted me up my brains fell out of the back of my head. Have a look."

He turned around. Jagged edges of skull framed a gaping hole in the back of his head, it looked like a window pane after a brick has gone through it.

Sid turned to face me, and then nodded at Dave's body. "He's on his way. Probably on fire as we speak. Nasty little cunt."

His cheeks hollowed as he drew on the Woodbine. "You better go," he said.

I put the pillow back on the chair. When I looked up, Sid was gone.

I took a moment to stroke Dave's head, felt myself smile as I whispered, "Fuck you," and then I walked out of the room.

*****

I joined the band and very soon Jimmy and I began writing together, and gradually we built up a decent repertoire of original, hard-driving songs.

Without his thug twin for back up, Alex left me alone. But he still hated my guts, and I hated his. There was still a score to be settled, but I bided my time.

In 1976, The Sex Pistols (or Malcom Maclaren's Monkees, as I called them) hit the UK like a lightning bolt, sparking a wildfire that swept across the country.

By 1977 our back catalogue captured the zeitgeist perfectly and we were soon compared with The Pistols, The Clash and The Stranglers.

Our name began to spread. A demo tape played by John Peel begat a local radio interview, which begat more gigs, which begat an offer of a deal with an up and coming indie record company, which begat a hit single, which begat another one, and another one.

And then we hit the big time.

We did Top of The Pops three times, became regulars on the John Peel show, and even supported the Rolling Stones for one show (John Lee Hooker was ill and we happened to be the only band in town. But still…).

After the Stones gig, Keith Richards asked if he could play my guitar. When he picked up El Diablo, he looked at me sideways, chuckled and then winked knowingly as he played the opening riff to Sympathy for the Devil.

Later that night, Keith posed for a picture with me. Later still, his dealer introduced me to heroin.

We made it onto the covers of New Musical Express, Melody Maker and Smash Hits.

All through this El Diablo never left my side, and never let me down. She became my trademark, and part of music lore, almost as famous as BB King's 'Lucille'. I made sure she was on every album cover, picture disc and concert poster.

Gibson got to hear of it and offered to give me a real SG, and a very lucrative sponsorship deal that would've set me up for life, provided that I agree to get rid of El Diablo. I declined, which sent Alex over the top in a thermonuclear drunken hissy fit.

"Are you fucking mad?" He screamed. "The biggest guitar company in the world have offered to give you one of their guitars, and you'd rather play that cheap piece of shit?" His foot lashed out, kicking El Diablo from her stand

Even though I'd killed two people, Alex Scott was the first and last person that I had ever punched. Drawing on a lifetime of experience, I knew exactly where to hit him. The first punch broke his nose, the second his cheekbone, the third and fourth resulted later in an eye-watering bill for cosmetic dentistry and the kicks to his nuts made him scream like baby.

That was in the Green Room at the BBC studios, just before we played on The Old Grey Whistle Test, which explains why Alex didn't appear that night.

A week later, a couple of days before Christmas, we played the legendary gig in Belfast.

I hadn't seen Alex since I smacked him. He flew to Belfast on his own, joining us for the sound check before the gig. He didn't speak to anyone, and no one spoke to him.

I felt nervous at being there. We were an English band playing in Belfast at the height of The

Troubles, and you could feel the tension in the venue. But we played a storm, the crowd roared their approval at every song. Half way through the set, Mick was introducing the band like he always did, when Alex stalked across the stage, grabbed the microphone and pointed to me.

"And this little shit is our lead guitarist. The IRA blew up his brother, and if any of you lot are in tonight I'll buy you all a drink."

El Diablo buzzed in my hand. Its devil-shape burned behind my eyelids.

Half the crowd cheered, the other half booed. And then it all kicked off. All of us had to duck as a hail of bottles and broken seats clattered onto the stage.

Mick froze centre-stage. I can't say I blame him.

Jimmy came across to me. "We've got to do something," he yelled. "This is like the Stones at fucking Altamont."

I played a familiar riff. Jimmy nodded, patted me on the shoulder, and then looked at Tom.

"Stiff Little Fingers," he shouted.

Tom nodded. Mick looked petrified. "I don't know any," he said.

Jimmy shrugged. "I fucking do." He stepped forward to his mic, "1-2-3-4…!"

I played the riff again, and the crowd roared as we thundered through a monster version of "Alternative Ulster".

When we finished, the house lights came on and I saw the full extent of the ongoing carnage. The auditorium was a frenzied mass of vicious sectarian fighting. In the midst of the violence I saw a familiar face battling his way to the exit.

It was to be our last ever gig.

Backstage was chaos and the band got separated in the melee. When we all made it back to the dressing room, Alex was nowhere to be seen. The unspoken assumption was that he'd made his own way to wherever he was going.

Jimmy looked at me. "What he said was out of order. Are you OK?"

I said I was fine.

El Diablo continued buzzing in my hand, and in my mind.

Alex's body was found three days later. He'd been shot through both knees and through the back of the head. His hooded body left next to a burnt-out car on a patch of wasteland in Bandit Country.

The Turtle Doves split up after the Belfast gig, I haven't seen them since.

After that I bummed around. When a solo career didn't work out, I did some session work and got by. And then my mum died of cancer, I lost interest in everything, and that's when my habit really got a hold of me.

When you're in the money, a heroin addiction is something you can manage. Something you can laugh off, or justify to yourself. When I stopped earning, my life spiraled into a nosedive towards yet another "Live Fast, Die Young" rock and roll cliché.

Looking back I've forgotten more than I can recall. Can't even remember the last time I played. Every last piece of my music memorabilia has gone now. Squirted through a filthy syringe to give me ever-shortened bouts of blessed oblivion.

All I had left was my guitar. I tried to pawn it the other day. The pawnbroker laughed at me as he offered me a pittance, and then laughed even louder as I stumbled out onto the street. People can smell desperation, and when you're a fallen rock star and drug addict the only place you'll find sympathy is in the dictionary, somewhere between shit and syphilis.

Most of my veins have collapsed now, I'm half blind (injecting yourself through the eye will do that), my teeth are rotten and I've got ulcers all over my body. My worldly possessions are this notebook, a pen that I nicked from a betting shop, a sleeping bag and the clothes that are hanging off me.

And that fucking guitar. Still burning red and as immaculate as the day I bought it, while my life has turned to shit.

This morning I woke up under some bushes. At least it didn't rain in the night. One of the newspapers I'm lying on is a couple of days old. The front-page story is about a British Army patrol killed by the IRA in Londonderry. There are pictures of the victims, one of whom is Shaven-Headed Guy,

AKA the late Sergeant Major Adam Lane, 2nd Battalion, The Parachute Regiment. Best friend of my late brother, and pall-bearer at his funeral.

The last time I saw him we were standing over the body of Alex Scott, Adam's Browning 9mm still smoking in my hand. Adam had broken both of Alex's ankles so that he couldn't make a run for it – he was good at breaking bones, was Adam – and then told me where to shoot him, to make it look like a punishment shooting.

Alex screamed like a baby, said he was sorry for all the times he and his brother beat me up, snot pouring down his face as he begged for mercy. I was as high as a kite but I remember laughing when I blew his kneecaps out, and the stench of him shitting himself when pulled the hood over his face and pushed the gun barrel against the back of his head.

After a lifetime of imagining scenarios of slow, violent revenge, I thought killing the Scott twins would make me feel better. Instead, all of my dark fantasies of retribution turned into terrifying nightmares of remorse - hideous dreams from which

I always wake screaming. And when I go for too long without a heroin fix, my night terrors appear as daylight hallucinations.

The gift that keeps on giving.

When I'm not high or hallucinating I think of Sid the milkman, how it felt to batter his head on the pavement, cracking it open until his brains leaked out.

Lately, I've seen him every day. Sometimes he talks to me, but mostly he stands to one side, a Woodbine in his mouth, blowing smoke rings, smiling quietly, looking at his watch and biding his time.

I realise that I've shit myself in my sleep. I pick up the damp newspaper and read the story about the IRA bomb.

Sid's waving to me now, beckoning me towards him. I guess it's time to go. I stand up, and sling El Diablo's strap over my shoulder for one last performance.

As I stagger towards Sid, the railway line's vibrating and I can hear the train a'coming.

"It's a Friday," said Sid. "Everyone always pays their bills on a Friday."

Prison Trilogy

The next three stories first appeared in Five Pairs of Shorts. Each of them was inspired by writing prompts suggested by members of a top-secret writing group that I once belonged to. I've been meaning to expand them further, maybe as a novel or screenplay. I just haven't got round to it yet.

338

Terry – Part One

It was two-fifteen in the afternoon when I heard the news.

Harry-the-blade had passed the message that he wanted a meeting; and when Harry says jump, you don't just say, "how high?", you don't come back down unless he says so.

You do not want to upset Harry-the-blade.

My name's Terry. I was part of the gang that robbed the two security vans up the West-end.

There was four of us: me, Harry, Right-handed-Ronnie and Mickey-the-squeeze. Harry got fifteen years in a maximum-security place up north while me, Ronnie and Mickey were banged up together in this dump. They each got a ten stretch; it was my first offence and I had a good lawyer so I got away with five years.

That was two years ago and I learned early on that I don't ever want to get banged up again. The end was in sight now and when Harry showed up last week - somehow he'd wangled a transfer down here - I must admit I had mixed feelings, but there you are.

I got to the exercise yard at two o'clock sharp and stood next to the fence, shivering in the biting cold February wind.

Ten minutes later I saw Harry sauntering across the yard, cons moving out of his way like he was a leaf-blower. Usually he was flanked by Ronnie and Mickey flying in close formation, today he was alone. He walked up close and said he wanted a fag.

Fags are currency but when Harry says he wants something, it's in your interests to oblige. I opened the packet, pulled one out, lit it with mine and gave it to him. He rewarded me with a nod and that simple, slight movement was enough to make me feel good.

See, when you're world is being locked into a nine-by-nine cell for eighteen hours a day with half an hour outside, rain or shine, day in-day out, you need all the friends you can get. And believe me, a nod from Harry-the-blade feels very friendly indeed.

It's all relative.

Harry took a long drag, his eyes never leaving mine. "Bit o'news, Terry," he said. "We're going out."

I must have looked stupid because he said, "You, me, Ronnie and Mickey, we're going over the wall."

"What do you mean?" I said.

"There's a maintenance team comin' in to dig up some drains by the kitchens. Arrangements have been made and we're gonna be smuggled out in their van." His lips parted to reveal teeth like gravestones in an abandoned cemetery. It was as close to a smile as you got with Harry. "We're breakin' out, Terry lad."

I forced a deadpan expression. This was the last thing I wanted to hear.

Harry tapped the side of his nose. "Got another job lined up, sure-fire winner, better than any pension. Been goin' through it for a few days now, all the details are in Mickey's cell."

He slapped me on the shoulder, "Be just like old times, Terry lad."

You don't want to argue with Harry-the-blade so I smiled and said, "Cool, when's it gonna happen?"

"Wednesday night," he said. "I've jacked us all up with kitchen duty, doors are gonna be left open and we're gonna slip out and hide in the van. It ain't gonna get searched on the on the way out, it's all been sorted. I got connections."

Harry's influence was legendary, but this was fast work, even for him.

He told me where I had to be and when, then turned and walked off. I watched as respectful cons moved out of his way, some of them casting furtive looks in my direction.

My mind was reeling. Most cons who escape end up getting caught. But then, Harry isn't like most cons.

All the same, I didn't sleep after that, just kept thinking about what was about to happen and what my options were.

I kept to myself for the next few days, hardly left my cell. Then, on Wednesday morning, all hell broke loose. I heard an alarm kick off, then people running and shouting and then a screw appeared in my doorway.

I stood up, tried to act calm, my heart thumping as he looked at me.

"Lock down," he said.

Then the door slammed shut. Sitting on my bunk, I listened to the angry shouts of cons locked in their cells, my thoughts racing as I wondered what was happening.

I heard approaching footsteps, heard them stop and I stood up as someone unlocked my door and swung it open.

"Visitor for you, Terry."

The screw stepped aside, nodded respectfully as Harry-the-blade walked in, then closed the door behind him.

"Hello Terry," said Harry.

"What's happening, Harry?"

"Mickey's cell's been turned over."

His first punch put me down, the second one broke my nose. Harry ripped my shirt apart then leaned in close, engulfing me in prison breath. "Five years for armed robbery in my gang? I don't think so. I knew you was a fucking grass but I had to make sure. I told Mickey it was tomorrow and told Ronnie it was Friday. You sang like a fuckin' canary, dincha?"

A blade appeared and with two deft swipes Harry extended my smile up to my cheekbones then reached inside, sliced off my tongue and stuffed my shirt into my mouth.

Agony filled my world and I swallowed blood as I screamed behind the gag.

Harry just smiled. "Thoughtchoo was due for parole, dincha? Fucking dream on."

I screamed again as Harry placed the blade against my eye, then he grinned and patted my cheek. "That's enough for now, but this ain't over. You an" me, we're gonna have some fun."

Harry smiled and stood up, "I think this is yours."

I felt my tongue hit my forehead.

You upset me, Terry," he said. "And you do not want to upset Harry-the-blade."

Mickey the Squeeze

My only regret is that I didn't do anything sooner.

My name is Mickey Jupp, most people know me as Mickey-the-squeeze. I'm doing a ten-stretch for my part in robbing the two security vans up the West-end. There was me, Terry, Harry-the-blade and Right-handed-Ronnie.

They call me Mickey-the-squeeze because of the methods I use to get information out of people. You'd be surprised how cooperative someone becomes when you've got their right hand in a vice.

Or their head.

I've done that more times than I care to mention and it always ends the same way. Even the hardest bastards you'll ever meet will spill the beans eventually, usually after begging and offering to give me their money, their houses, their wives and their daughters.

They all cried for their mothers, too. Every single one of them.

Sometimes, the first turn of the vice would be enough. Imagination would kick in and the poor, terrified bastard would tell us everything within thirty seconds. Harry would still insist on giving them the full treatment, taking it to its conclusion. Not many people survived it. Those who did were never the same again.

I'm not proud of what I did and I can't change what I did. I wish to Christ that I could. All I can offer is that I don't do that anymore. I found God, you see.

I know what you're thinking.

Every con finds God, usually just before the parole board is due. Not me, I'm never applying for parole. Ten years is what I've got and ten years is what I'm going to do. Jesus spent forty days in the wilderness. Well, my wilderness in here and will last me until the time comes for me to leave. I'm OK with that, it's my penance. Every action has a consequence, a price to be paid, and I'm paying back now. I've found my peace and when my time comes to meet my maker I'm gonna walk tall, walk straight and look Him right in the eye. He'll understand.

What Harry did was bang out of order, Terry didn't deserve that. Thing is, once Harry gets an idea in his head then dynamite won't shift it and if part of that idea results in him taking a dislike to you then suddenly the world becomes a very small place. Harry was convinced that we got caught because Terry grassed us up in return for a reduced sentence. I don't think he did, Terry had a good lawyer and a bunch of references from people in some pretty high-up places. I've been banged up more times than I can count and I've only ever met one or two cons who really don't belong in jail. Terry was one of them. As the saying goes, if you can't do the time, don't do the crime. He found that out the hard way.

Granted, it was Terry who spilled the beans about the break-out story, but no one in here blames him for that. Harry told me and Ronnie the cxact same story but with different days. I know that because Ronnie approached ma afterwards. Harry didn't bank on that, he thought he could divide and conquer.

Me and Ronnie, we got wise to Harry and decided we'd had enough. Of course, we had to play along, make out like we was muckers; and we wandered around like we owned the gaff. And all the time we were working out what needed to be done. We tried to get word to Terry, to warn him not to say anything but he hardly left his cell.

Everyone knows Harry-the-blade and everyone understands why Terry did what he did. He kept his head down, did his time and was due for a parole hearing. Everyone knew that he would probably get it first shout and he wasn't going to give that up for anyone, he's got plans to turn his life around and we all know that he will, despite what happened to him.

Terry must be the first grass I've ever met who can walk around with a bunch of cons with his head held high. Mind, it's gonna be a long old road he's got to travel. He looked a bloody mess after Harry had finished with him; tore his face up proper and left the cell looking like a slaughterhouse.

The worst part was that Harry left instructions that no one was to go and help him until he said so. He wanted to make sure that Terry's face was as fucked up as it could be without killing him. Three hours the poor bastard lay there; lucky he didn't bleed out.

Harry, meanwhile, was in his cell getting a blowjob from his latest bitch whilst watching Goodfella's. Extreme violence always made him horny.

What he did to Terry was the last straw, something had to be done.

Harry's got more people in his pocket than anyone I've ever met, but he's not the only one. Ronnie knows a plastic surgeon in Harley Street who owes him a few favours. As soon as Terry is out of hospital, he's gonna have his face repaired for nothing. It's the least we could do.

That's only the start.

Word has gone around the prison; everyone's getting together in little groups and sharing everything they know about Harry-the-blade and his network. Me and Ronnie are gonna take this information and get things sorted. If all goes to plan, then every bent judge, copper and screw working for Harry are going to get a wake-up call. So far, there's a long list of some very important names. I wouldn't be surprised if it makes the papers.

Harry's time is over, no one's scared of him anymore.

My name is Mickey Jupp. Most people know me as Mickey-the-squeeze.

I'm the one who killed Harry-the-blade. My only regret is that I didn't do it sooner.

Terry – Part Two

"A man walks down the street, he doesn't where he's going...no,wait, he walks into a bar, that's it…"

Ronnie Townshend was rubbish at telling jokes. He tried telling that one just before we set off to rob the two security vans up the West-end.

Back then, he was one of those blokes who tried too hard to be funny. You know the sort I mean? You get one in every group, desperate to be popular, desperate to be one of the lads.

Classic sign of insecurity, so they say.

Harry-the-blade said Ronnie was a wanker, called him 'Right-handed Ronnie' so of course Mickey and me, we had to laugh.

I felt sorry for him. Everyone thought Ronnie wasn't all there.

Big mistake.

Ronnie Townshend is one of the sharpest blokes I've ever met. Trouble was, back then Harry kept him slapped down so he wouldn't allow himself to believe it.

Ronnie looked after me after Harry carved up my face and I won't ever forget that.

I can see now that Ronnie has a knack for forward thinking, being able to 'look at the big picture' or whatever it is those management pricks say.

I nearly became a management prick myself. I was all set to do a degree in business studies, a teacher even managed to get me work-experience at some posh bank in Canary Wharf.

Tell you what, one week amongst those fuckers was enough for me. Sharks they are, all of 'em. Sharks in expensive suits, morally dead and proud of it. Fuck doing that for the rest of my life.

I jacked it all in and got a job as a barman at Harry's local; that's where I met the rest of the gang. Obviously I knew they were villains, it was that sort of area, but it was a million miles from the false wankers at Canary Wharf.

Don't get me wrong, it wasn't Disneyworld, I was trading one bunch of sharks for another ten times more dangerous, but at least you felt alive.

One day, this punter started coming into the pub. He kept to himself at first but then started asking me questions about Harry and the gang. Of course, I told Harry straightaway.

Turns out he was an undercover cop, and not a very good one. They found his body in the Thames, his head crushed almost flat. How Mickey kept doing that is beyond me.

"Just like cracking walnuts, Terry," he told me. "Do it right and the top of the head splits right open."

He told me it never bothered him, but Ronnie told me Mickey used to get bad dreams and wake up crying.

Then he found God in E-Wing.

Anyway, a few nights later Harry came up to me in the pub. "Got a job coming up, Terry," he said. "Be a bit of pocket money for you."

So that's how I got in.

Back then it was a real buzz. I was a kid, I didn't know any better. Being banged-up soon changed that, I'm older and much, much wiser now.

So far, I have had two operations; the plastic surgeon reckons one more will fix my face so that I won't look like The Joker anymore. Couldn't do anything about my tongue, left it too long, they said.

Ronnie got me an iPad with a voice app. He's also sorted out a speech therapist too, for when I'm fit again. I think he feels guilty that Harry pegged me as the grass. Shit happens, I can understand Harry thinking it was me.

I must admit I smiled when I found out it was Ronnie. I reckon when the cops separated him from Harry, that's when he woke up and began to think for himself.

Ronnie could have grassed and got away without a conviction, but he knew if he'd done that, Harry would have found him. So, to make it look kosher, his deal was that he would go down with a proper sentence but get parole first shout. He knew that the cops wanted Harry big time, wanted him enough to offer Ronnie a rock-solid deal.

It was a ballsy move but Ronnie had his eye on the prize; he would use the time to make his plan, map out the big picture. Christ, it must have felt like a lottery win when Harry wangled that transfer.

The rest is history. Harry jumped me, Mickey killed Harry. A few weeks later, me and Ronnie got parole. I heard on the grapevine that Mickey lost it after Ronnie left, he confessed to killing Harry, tried to hang himself then got moved to the psychiatric wing.

Just goes to show. All this time everyone thought Ronnie wasn't all there, turns out he was the smartest of the lot.

Ronnie has taken over from Harry but things are different now, like chalk and cheese. See, Ronnie listens to people, treats them with respect - at first. Try and cross him after that and the gloves come off. It seems like every day he comes up with a thought or says something that blows your mind and peels back another tiny layer to reveal how his mind works.

The other day, the iPad reminded him about the gag he tried to tell just before we all got nicked.

"What gag was that, Terry?" he said.

"A man walks down the street. He doesn't know where he's going...no wait, he walks into a bar, that's it.."

"What was that all about?" said the iPad.

Ronnie winked at me, "Whatchoo think it was about?"

Then he asked me to join him when I'm fit again. Said he wants a business partner, someone with a bit of nous, someone he can trust.

The iPad said I was in.

Ronnie paused, smiled, winked slowly and said, "Perhaps you can be my right-hand man, Terry."

I think that was his idea of a joke.

Weight Watcher

*This was inspired by a filthy naval ditty, sung to the tune of
the Mariachi song, Cielito Lindo, in which Belinda does
something unspeakable to her brother's sombrero.*

My sister Belinda,
While cleaning the window,
Fell out with a scream and a thud.
As she lay in a daze,
She was shocked and amazed
At the impression she'd left in the mud.

"Climbing out of the crater,"
She remarked to me later
"Was a moment of personal disquiet,"
For such was the dent
From her rapid descent
She thought, "Maybe it's time for a diet."

After looking around
A solution was found
With a slogan she saw on a bus
"Are you overweight?
It's never too late,
To contact Bloaters R Us!"

So when she got home
She picked up the phone
Her heart was rapidly beating
A young girl named Joyce
With a nice friendly voice
Helped Belinda arrange her first meeting.

It was doomed from the start
And with heavy heart
My sister conceded defeat.
Three weeks of starvation
And humiliation
Caused Belinda to vote with her feet.

Twelve months have now passed
She's still a big lass
But Belinda, she couldn't care less
She's married to Stan
A thoughtful young man
Unconcerned with the size of her dress

Now my sister Belinda
Renewed her agenda
And no longer desires to be leaner
'Cos the wonderful man
Who shares her life plan
Is also the town window cleaner.

The Scoundrel and the Barmaid

This was inspired by the structure of the poem, 'Have a Nice Day' by Spike Milligan.

Said the man at the bar, "*My wife's left me.*"
Said the barmaid, "*I'm sorry to hear.*"
Said the man at the bar, "*She's been having,*
illicit liaisons I fear."

Said the barmaid, "*Who's she been seeing?*"
Said the man at the bar, "*Well, my dear,*
We've been having a new boiler fitted,
She's run off with the gas engineer."

Said the barmaid, "*That's terrible news.*"
Said the man at the bar, "*You don't say?*
My new boiler is still in its wrapper,
The house has been freezing for days."

Said the barmaid, "*The drinks are on me.*"
Said the man at the bar, "*Very kind,*
I'll have another large whiskey,
If you're sure that you really don't mind."

Said the barmaid, "*How do you feel now?*"
Said the man at the bar, "*Can't complain,*
It's not the first time she's done it,
No doubt she'll do it again."

Said the barmaid, "*Why do you put up with,*
the philandering ways of your wife?"
Said the man at the bar, "*The variety*

adds a great deal of spice to our life."

"Furthermore," said the man at the bar,
   "We got married for better or worse,
   And she doesn't know I've been sleeping,
   With a rather attractive young nurse."

Said the barmaid, *"You're as bad as each other."*
   Said the man at the bar, *"I agree,*
      but life is not a rehearsal,
   By the way, what time are you free?"

So the man at the bar and the barmaid,
   That night staggered back to her house.
      Now let's draw a veil,
      Over this sorry tale
Of a scoundrel and his wayward spouse.

Fat Man Blues

A poem about a novel. It can be found on YouTube, narrated by the superb American writer, Michael Clark.

Well I was sitting in a juke joint
In Clarksdale, Mississippi,
Just minding my own business
And getting high on booze,
When in walked this old white boy
Said his accent came from England,
Said he'd come to Mississippi
Come to see the delta blues,

I said there ain't no delta blues
No more in Clarksdale, Mississippi,
Cos it ain't nothin' but a theme park
For white folks just like you
But if you come along with me
I can show you where it happens
I can take you to a place where they play the real
blues

So then I dropped some names
Like Charley Patton and Robert Johnson
And the white boy looked at me
Like something just come loose
He said 'those old boys are dead'
I said that's a matter of opinion
And then I made an offer
That he could not refuse

See, the white boy had a poison
That was growing deep inside him
And I knew his clock was ticking
Knew his time would soon run out
So I laid it on the table
Told him I could fix his problem
If he'd come along with me,
There was never any doubt

So I took out all the poison
And we met up at the crossroads
And I tuned the white boy's gittar
And I said the deal was done
Then I took him back in time
To 1930s Mississippi
Where he walked the delta land
And went looking for some fun

Now White Boy he was happy
To be walkin' Mississippi
What he don't know didn't hurt him
He had nothin' left to lose
But be careful what you wish for
Cos the devil's in the detail
And you better read the small print
Of the Fat Man Blues

Someday

Inspired by the song, 'Someday' by Steve Earle.

There's gotta be more to life than this.

Earle Beauregard creaked the wooden chair onto its back legs and adjusted his baseball cap to shield the glare from the afternoon sun beating down on the dilapidated filling station.

Some filling station, two ancient pumps and falling-down wooden shack.

Texaco it was not.

The high point of his day - no, scratch that - the high point of his week so far had been the conversation with his last customer, an ignorant fat fuck wearing Ray-Ban Aviators and driving a shit box '79 Trans Am with Michigan plates and a busted muffler that made a sound like Satan clearing his throat.

Earle filled the tank while fat fuck used what passed for the bathroom.

Something wasn't right.

When fat fuck returned, Earle said, "this sure

don' look like no stock Trans Am, what-all yo' got under the hood?"

No reply.

Earle kept going. "I got me a '67 Chevelle, my daddy's car. Someday she gon' take me away from all this." He glanced at the plates and tried again. "Michigan, huh? Yo' sure are a long way from home."

The fat fuck removed his shades to reveal cold, dead eyes. "An' yo' sure are a long way away from anything that's yo' goddam business. All I wantchoo t' do is put gasoline in my goddam car."

Earle shrugged then slowed the pump as he topped off the tank. "That'll be twenty-five dollars."

Fat fuck handed over two tens and a five, got into the car and then leaned his head out of the window. "How far'r we from Memphis?"

Earle pointed on down the road. "Interstate's three miles that a-way, get on it an' head south fo' sixty miles.

Fat fuck grunted then spun the tires and roared away, the rasping, crackling snarl of the hopped-up Trans Am taking a long time to fade into the distance.

"Y'all have a nice day, now." Said Earle.

That was an hour ago.

Earle sighed. Twenty-four years old and pumpin' gas on a nowhere road in Shithole, Tennessee. There's gotta be a better way.

In the oppressive heat, his eyelids grew heavy to the drowsy, half-hearted buzz of insects; the only sound on the deserted road.

The door slam woke him up.

Earle opened his eyes to see a Tennessee state trooper standing next to a Ford Crown Vic' Interceptor.

"He'p yo', officer?"

The trooper removed his mirrored sunglasses. "Yo' work here, son?"

A dozen smart-ass replies flashed in Earle's head.

"Yes sir, I do," he said. "This place b'long to mah uncle."

"Anyone come past in the last hour or so?"

"No sir, been pretty quiet today."

Earle heard the words come out but had no

idea why he said them.

"Yo' sure 'bout that?" said the cop.

Earle pretended to think. "Well, I been working inside earlier, s'pose someone could have drove past then, but ain' nobody stopped here."

The state trooper stared at him for a long time, looked around, stared some more and said finally, "well, we're looking for a white male, five-ten, weighs about two hunnerd 'n' eighty pounds, drives a beat up ol' '79 Trans Am that sounds like a P.O.S."

Earle held the policeman's stare. "Well, I guess I'd remember seein' anyone like that."

The cop handed Earle a card. "Well, if yo' remember anything else, or see anything, call this number."

Turning the card over in his hand, Earle said, "What's he done?"

"He's a mean sumbitch," said the cop. "An' tha's all you need t'know. If yo' see him, jus' call that number."

A month later, Earle's uncle announced that he was closing the filling station.

Earle was locking up the place on the last day

when he heard the far-off roar of a high-performance engine. Running to the side of the road, he looked to his left and saw sunlight glinting off a shape emerging from the heat shimmer hovering above the tree-lined road. The shape grew larger and then...

"GOD-DAM!" Earle whooped in delight as the Trans Am blew past at better than a hundred and twenty, howling like a banshee and whipping up dust and road litter in its wake.

His senses reeling, Earle watched the taillights disappear, listened to the falling note of the engine and then heard the squeal of rubber and dull crumple and crash-tinkle of a car going end-over-end.

Earle sprinted around to the rear of the shack, jumped into his black Chevelle, gunned the engine and fishtailed onto the road.

He found the Trans Am half a mile away, nose-down in a drainage ditch. In the middle of the road a large cardboard box had burst open, spilling out about a dozen clear plastic bags.

Earle stopped the car and got out. Inside each bag were hundreds of white pills, Earle put everything into the Chevelle's trunk and went to check the Trans Am.

Bracing himself with one foot on the open driver's door, Earle looked inside.

It was a mess.

Barely conscious, fat fuck hung from his seat-belt, blood trickling from his nose. Wedged between the windshield and the dashboard was a black leather attaché case. Earle balanced it on the steering wheel, flicked the clasps, opened it and whistled when he saw the thick bundles of hundred-dollar bills. Along with the cash was a notebook, Earle rifled through pages of names and phone numbers then put it back and shut the case.

A quick look inside confirmed that the Trans Am was empty; whatever was in the passenger glove box could stay there.

Fat fuck groaned as Earle frisked him to discover a cellphone in his shirt pocket and a Smith and Wesson .38 in his waistband. Pocketing the cellphone, he spun the chamber of the .38 then grabbed the case and clambered away from the ditch.

Standing on the road, Earle Beauregard stared down at the Trans Am, lifted the .38, blew fat fuck's head apart and then climbed into the Chevelle.

Buddha

A Buddhist went to heaven,

And saw that God lived there,

He met St Peter at the gate,

But could only stand and stare,

For a lifetime of devotion,

To the teachings of Gautama,

Had left the faithful monk,

In a state of mental trauma,

As God approached the Buddhist,

These words the old monk uttered:

"So it is you after all,

I can't believe that it's not Buddha..."

Thomas Green the Submarine

I felt an urge to write a nonsense poem, and while driving to work the phrase 'Thomas Green the Submarine' popped into my head. I wrote it in about twenty minutes. It has since been brought to life by Half Deaf Clatch who narrated it for a video on YouTube.

A troubled lad named Thomas Green,
Claimed to be a submarine.
His father said, "Son, don't be daft,
to be an underwater craft,
You must be steel, not flesh and blood.
Submerged, you'll not do very good,
How long d'you think you'll hold your breath?
The water's cold, you'll catch your death,
Come on Thomas, eat your tea,
Let's speak no more of the undersea."

Tom listened to his father scoff,
Refused to let it put him off,
He eyed his dad with naked scorn,
And then declared, "We dive at dawn!"

The cheeky lad was sent to bed,
and when he'd gone his father said,
"A submarine? The thought's absurd.
That boy's not right, you mark my words."
His mother sighed, "Oh leave him be.
It's just a phase, you wait and see."

Next day they went to wake their son,
But found that Thomas Green had gone.
Police were called, the search commenced,
To find the lad their vowed intent.
They searched for days to no avail.
His tear-stained folks, distraught and pale,
pleaded for his safe return,
but mum and dad would later learn,
that while they cried on live TV,
Thomas Green had put to sea.

The first event that got them thinking,
Was news of the channel ferry sinking.
"Mystery Blast!" the newsreader said.
"We don't know yet how many's dead.
And this just in! I'll hand you over,

To our man, who's down in Dover."
The news reporter, a handsome hunk,
Cried out, "Another ship's been sunk!
The navy's on their way with divers,
To see if they can find survivors."

It didn't stop there and on live TV,
Tom carried out a wolf pack spree.
Two more ships sank 'neath the waves,
Creating two more watery graves.
As they stared at the telly screen,
Shell-shocked, Mr. and Mrs Green,
Put together two and two,
And said, "Looks like we're in the poo.
They'll think our standards must be slipping,
To let our son sink merchant shipping."

The Royal Navy arrived on scene,
And began the hunt for Thomas Green,
But Thomas, without fear or barrier,
Sank their brand-new aircraft carrier.
The captain yelled, "All hands on deck!"
Mr. Green yelled, "Flippin' 'eck!

This has gone beyond a joke,
They'll not like that, those navy folk."
And he was right, they weren't impressed,
To lose a ship, their Sunday best.

The navy said, "Enough's enough."
The gloves came off, they acted tough.
A frigate with a huge depth charge
Arrived on scene and gave it large,
Stirring up a huge maelstrom,
In the search for U-Boat Tom.
The explosion made the water boil,
Then came the tell-tale slick of oil.
Then all was quiet on the briny scene.
Was this the end of Thomas Green?

A few months on, the fuss died down.
The Greens moved to another town,
Of their son they heard not a thing,
Until one day the doorbell ring.
A parcel in the letter flap,
A puzzled Mr. Green unwrapped,
And there, inside a plastic bag,

A Jolly Roger pirate flag.
Still out at sea on a secret mission,
Submarine Tom is no longer missing

Latin Limerick

A few years ago I was challenged to write a limerick that included a Latin phrase. This still makes me chuckle.

A callow young farmer from Leominster,

Paid a whore and attempted to enter,

But on him was the joke,

For the whore was a bloke,

Who winked and said,

"Caveat Emptor"

The Owl & the Pussycat

A 21st Century take on an old classic (with apologies to Edward Lear).

The owl and the pussy cat went to sea

In a beautiful, pea-green boat

They sailed past Dover

And were swiftly pulled over

By HM Customs afloat

T'was a miserable caper

For they had no papers

To prove the land they were from

And with a brisk rubber stamp

They were sent to a camp

With others who seek asylum

The owl looked up to the stars above

And sang to a small guitar

"Oh customs man, oh customs official

What a stupid official you are, you are

What a stupid official you are."

Official said to the owl,

"You ill-tempered fowl

You sewer-mouthed so and so

We had no way of knowing

Which way you were going

I'm just doing my job, you know

And oh how we laughed

at your pea-green craft

you must take us for mugs

a bird and a feline?

Adrift in a sea-lane?

We stopped you to search for drugs, for drugs

We stopped you to search for drugs

And then he took them away

For half a year and a day

To a place they called Heathrow

He said "Oh prisoners of mine,

This is your quarantine,

For the next six months,

This is your home.

Now don't cry like babies,

For we don't want rabies,

In the land where the oak trees grow,

As pets with no owners,

On you is the onus,

I don't make the rules, you know, you know,

I don't make the rules you know."

Protesting their crime

The two did their time

And the six months crawled slowly by

And on the last day at 3

They were finally set free

By a pig who lived in a sty

On the day of release-a,

They dined on a pizza,

And ice-cream that they ate

with a spoon.

And then wing in paw,

Along the M4,

They danced by the light of the moon the, moon

They danced by the light of the moon.

The Ghost of the Blues

I wrote this in 2003, and was thrilled when German musician, Werner Lindner asked if he could record it. There's a video knocking around of his band playing it at a gig.

I walk these dusty roads forever

Wanderin' cross the Delta land

A mojo in my pocket

and a guitar in my hand

Born from poverty and hardship

Dark misery and shame

Now everybody's heard of me

Everybody knows my name

I was right there at the crossroads

The day the wind blew cold

When the first disciple made a deal

And the Devil bought his soul

Poor boy in Mississippi

Nowhere else to go but up

Strumming on street corners

For change in an old tin cup

Followers preach my message

Some find glory, wealth and fame

And some fall by the wayside

Dying early in my name

I'm the sound of hard rocks breaking

I'm the voice of the old chain gang

I'm the sound of a thousand ways

To mistreat your fellow man

I'm the wailing of a slide guitar

I'm the walk from town to town

I'm the hobo in the boxcar

I'm the railroad whistle's moan

I'm the cotton on the sharecrop

I'm the juke joint after dark

I'm the panicked, crashing through the woods

I'm the Sheriff's hound dog's bark

I'm the prejudice and anger

I'm the lynch mob's hangman's noose

I'm the song of desperation

I'm the ghost of the Delta Blues

See You in Church, White Boy

Yet more shameless self promotion for my novel, Fat Man Blues. This time in the form of a song.

In a church house,
by the crossroads,
Me and Fat Man,
We made a pact.
He said you're mine,
And mine alone,
Belong to me,
And that's a fact.

(chorus)
See you in Church, White Boy,
See you in church, is what he said to me,
See you in Church, White Boy,
Bring the blues back here to me.

"You ain't alive,
But you ain't dead,
I got something,
For you to see.
Walk the Delta,
Go find the blues,
Then bring 'em back,
Back here to me."

(chorus)
See you in Church, White Boy,
See you in church, is what he said to me,
See you in Church White Boy,
Bring the blues back here to me.

High Praise Indeed

Here are some kind words people have written about my

books.

Richard Wall's writing is explosive! It's like Tarantino set off a stick of dynamite next to a box of C4. Wall takes no prisoners in his stories of the American South.
Ran Walker – Author of The Last Bluesman

"Near Death shook me to the core. Lean prose. A propulsive, hard action and laugh out loud at times. A story written with heart, angst & grace. After a few pages not only was I hooked, but I became an instant fan of a sensational new voice in crime fiction. "
Mark Pelletier - #BookTalk, Santa Cruz,

California

"Richard Wall writes like a motherfucker…"
James Garside – Journalist, Author & Travel Writer

Richard Wall is one of the most exciting authors of our age. His writing grips you from start to finish and leaves you breathless.
Burning Chair Publishing

Acknowledgements

In which I attempt to give thanks for the support and encouragement I have received over the years from family, friends, and complete strangers from across the planet.

Firstly, my wife, Barbara, for putting up with me and for everything you do.
Kyle Sweet, my long-time friend, and drinking partner on that fateful night in Clarksdale, Mississippi during which my novel, FAT MAN BLUES was conceived.
Ran Walker, a phenomenal writer whose wisdom knows no bounds, and whose friendship is priceless.
Andrew McLatchie (aka Half Deaf Clatch) for being so damn cool. Michael Clark for narrating my words.
Matty-Bob Cash and Emma Dehaney at Burdizzo Books and Mark Pelletier from #BookTalk on Twitter, for their tireless promotion of indie writers.
Pete Oxley and Simon Finnie at Burning Chair Publishing. Shipmates: Dave Gildea, Phil Howell, Stu Cox, Jim Paine, Nigel Fawcett and Terry Clarke.
Musicians: Ray Mytton, Trevor 'Babajack' Steger, Gary Tolley, Scott Wainwright, Tanya Piche, and Barry 'Blues Barn' Hopwood.
Belated thanks to Kizzy Thomson – you did your best!
And finally, every single person who has taken the time to read my words, buy my books, leave a review or recommend me to someone else – you're all fabulous and I can't thank you enough.

Thanks for watching. See you on the other side…

Printed in Great Britain
by Amazon